Redeemed

Safe Havens 3

Sandy James

Cover design by Dragonfly Press Design
www.dragonflypressdesign.com
Book design by Sandy James
Published by James Gang Publishing

Sandy James
sandyjames.com

Printed in the United States of America
First Printing: January 2014
ISBN: 978-1940295060

Chapter One

Denver, Colorado—September 1884

Sara Fuller gave one last look to the drunken cowboy passed out on her bed.

He was older—at least a handful of years over her own twenty-one. At least he'd paid for a bath and a shave, which was more than most men did before they came to The Palace. This one had a few manners. The one before had delivered a hit that had set her eye to throbbing.

Drake, the man in her bed, had just returned from a long drive. He'd scooped up his considerable pay, got something decent to eat and a bath, then he came right to Crazy Kate's brothel for what he'd missed most while on the trail.

Sara had hit the jackpot when she'd rifled through his pack. Not only did he have his own pay. He was evidently a foreman, because she'd found the entire payroll, a sum so staggering she almost changed her mind about stealing it. Then she'd found her courage and gone right ahead with her plan. Drake would just have to explain it to his bosses.

At least he'd been more of a lover than most customers, treating her like a lady instead of a whore. But that was exactly what she was.

A whore.

The urge to spit on him as though he were all of her former customers was overwhelming, but she denied herself that last insult. With her luck, he'd awaken and blacken her left eye to match her right. Of course, most of the men who came to her room got a little rough. A bruise here. A scrape there. At least she'd avoided the broken bones some of the other girls got.

Besides, if she indulged herself, he might wake up and ruin her escape.

After adding the bills she'd stolen to her own nest egg, she stuffed the cash into her carpetbag along with the letter that had started her plan of escape. Then she donned her clothing, buttoning the crisp, white blouse all the way to the throat. When she left, she'd go looking like a lady. Prim skirt. Starched shirt. Sensible boots.

No one would ever guess what she truly was.

Was, she reminded herself. The money she'd just fleeced from the cowboy would get her away from Denver. For good.

As she reached for the doorknob, Sara cast one last glance around the room. The familiar brass bed. The oak bureau. The cracked pitcher and porcelain basin. There was nothing here for her now. No good memories. No fond farewells. Only pain and a life that nearly destroyed her pride.

The cowboy snorted and rolled to his side, making her heart leap and pound furiously. Thankfully, his movement was followed by more loud snoring. As much whisky as she'd poured down his throat, he'd be out for a good, long while—at least long enough for her to get her backside to Union station.

She'd been watching the trains for weeks, plotting the timing of her escape. She'd have to finish the journey on a stagecoach, but a train would see her safely away before her last customer could ever find her. A twinge of guilt was brushed aside. While he might have worked hard weeks on the trail to earn that windfall and had been entrusted with the men's pay, she'd worked harder on her back the last six months. He could make more on his next long drive and explain the loss of the payroll to his boss. If she stayed here, she'd be dead before she reached thirty.

Sara closed the door and tread softly down the stairs.

"Yer really goin', girl?" Crazy Kate McCoy rubbed a cloth over the now empty bar and narrowed her eyes.

What a ridiculous question. All the girls who worked for Kate knew how much Sara wanted to go. They *all* wanted to get away.

Few ever would.

Now, Sara needed to find out if Kate would allow it. Although she was prepared for a fight, she hoped the madam would make this an easy escape. As fast as Kate's moods shifted, Sara had no idea what to expect.

She tried honesty. "I'm really going."

"And ye think I'll be lettin' ye go without a penalty?"

Sara lightly touched her swollen face. "I think that man yesterday gave me more than enough *penalty*."

Kate gave a scoffing laugh. "Aye...that's a nice shiner." Tossing the towel aside, she came from behind the bar. "There'll be no penalty. Ye've paid dearly enough." She gathered Sara into her arms and hugged her against her rather large body.

It was akin to being hugged by a fat bear wearing far too much cheap toilet water. Not knowing how to react to the unusual show of affection, Sara tried to relax and prayed that Crazy Kate wouldn't live up to her nickname and suddenly become mean.

Turning Sara loose, Kate reached into her pocket and yanked out a hefty wad of bills—no doubt the takings for the evening. With ten girls working in the brothel, the woman was raking in money from the miners and cowboys—even respectable businessmen—who found their way to the wrong side of Denver. She peeled off a few bills and handed them to Sara. "Get yerself away a'fore that bastard wakes, or ye'll be on yer back again. A proper stallion, that man be."

With a nod, Sara squeezed the money in her fist. She didn't dare open her carpetbag to put what Kate surrendered with the rest of her bounty. If Kate knew that Sara had just robbed that cowboy blind, she'd find herself lying dead in the alley. "Thank you, Kate."

"Be gone with ye." Kate waved her away with the back of her hand. "Get outta this godforsaken town a'fore it kills ye. Ye ain't got what it takes ta be a proper whore, Sara. Leave now while ye've got yer health and yer looks." Whirling around, she considered her own reflection in the cracked mirror behind the bar. A frown fixed on her painted lips, and her bloodshot eyes filled with tears. "Mine been gone far too long."

"Take care of yourself," Sara murmured as she strode to the door that led to the alley.

Kate never answered as she sadly touched her mirrored reflection with a shaky hand. Tears rolled down her rouged cheeks, and her bottom lip trembled. "I were a looker in my day. I truly were."

Afraid the unstable woman would grow angry, Sara slipped on her coat and left.

The moment her feet hit the cobblestones, she ran. Holding her reticule tight to her chest, she followed the path she knew well. At Union Station there was a train waiting to take her away. From Denver. From the life she'd led the last six months. From a future that was too grim to even consider.

If she didn't escape, she'd one day be the sad and defeated woman staring in the mirror and wondering when her soul had died.

A drizzling rain began to fall a block before the station. Sara kept running, ignoring the stitch in her side and trying to keep her footing as the walkways grew slippery. The harsh autumn weather matched her mood—dark and bleak. Her fear drove her forward.

Had the cowboy awakened?

Had Kate changed her mind?

Would someone come to stop her and fetch her back to The Palace?

No. I'll die if that happens.

She'd wanted to escape for so long. Forever. From the moment she'd found herself standing in front of Crazy Kate, knowing the woman owned her as though she were a slave and understanding what she'd have to do to survive.

Sara didn't remember buying the ticket. Nor did she remember boarding the train. By the time her senses returned, she sat on a day bench, looking out a filthy window and watching the scenery pass by in a blur until the buildings changed to houses and then to trees and wide open fields.

There were days of travel ahead, but that time was now her own. No customers. No Crazy Kate. No anything she didn't want to do.

I'm free!

For the first time in far too long, Sara allowed herself to smile.

***

Caleb plucked a piece of hay from one of the fragrant bales piled up outside of the livery. Crossing the street, he took a seat on the worn bench outside the general store and set the stalk in the corner of his mouth. Sure, it was a nasty habit. But chewing on hay stalks beat cheroots or cigars. As nasty habits went, his was mostly harmless.

He laid his outstretched arms against the back of the bench, settling in for his familiar wait as he wondered if he'd be going home alone. Again.

The sun was warm today, and he enjoyed the feel of it on his face. Closing his eyes, he stretched his legs out, crossing them at the ankles.

Today was the day. His heart told him so.

"Lord have mercy! You're here *again?*"

The voice belonged to his older brother, Gideon, so Caleb didn't bother to open his eyes. "Yep."

"Waiting for the damned stage, I suppose."

"Yep."

"When are you gonna get it through your thick skull that this plan of yours ain't gonna work? One letter ain't gonna convince a woman to marry you."

With a reluctant sigh, he opened his eyes and leveled a hard stare at his brother. "It'll work. Just you wait and see."

"Bullshit. Women don't wanna come live with lonely Montana farmers. That pastor lied to you, damn it. He ain't finding you a wife. You just pissed all that cash away, little brother."

Despite his brother's confidence that Caleb had wasted his money by giving it to Reverend Hayes, Caleb knew the good pastor was going to follow through. He'd use that money to send Caleb the wife he wanted. The wife he *needed*. She was coming to him—maybe even on the stage due in White Pines any minute.

Yes, she was coming to him.

Today.

Why was he so sure? Because he knew something Gideon didn't, which brought a smug smile to Caleb's lips. Someone had claimed the fare from Hayes—a woman who wanted a fresh start, or so the letter the reverend had sent told him.

Every morning for the last week, Caleb did his chores and then hitched up his wagon and drove to White Pines. He'd waited here at the general store, hoping his salvation would be on the next stage. And each day of disappointment had increased his anticipation until he was sure he'd see her soon or lose his mind.

Today, his gut told him. *She'll come today.*

She didn't have to be beautiful. She didn't even have to be pretty. Hell, she could be as ugly as his mule. All he desired was that she be young, healthy, and kind—and willing to come to the last vestiges of the frontier to become his wife.

"She'll come," Caleb said, his voice a harsh whisper.

When Gideon put his hand on Caleb's shoulder, it took all Caleb's self-control not to smack it away. "It's been too long, brother. Had a woman taken you up on your offer, she'd be here by now. You ain't heard nothing from the pastor."

Ah, but I have. "She'll come."

With a shake of his head, Gideon walked away. At least he was smart enough to know that nothing he could say would change Caleb's mind. He was getting a wife.

Even if he had to *buy* one.

Squinting, he stared into the distance, then he grinned as though it were Christmas morning.

The stage was coming.

Jumping to his feet, he spit the hay out and waited. Long minutes passed as the sweaty horses crossed the last of the distance to the general store on the street leading into the small town.

The anticipation was killing him the same way the loneliness had eaten at him. In all the time he'd waited, never had he felt so much confidence. She would step off the stagecoach, then she'd smile. He'd take her hand, and he'd lead the way to the church.

Such a simple plan.

The stage ground to a stop, clouds of dust following in its wake.

Caleb stood his ground.

The driver peered down from his perch, giving no indication of whether he knew why Caleb waited, even though he'd seen him there each day. With no comment, he climbed over the top, unhooked the thick ropes holding down the baggage, and started tossing things to the ground while his companion crawled down the side of the coach.

The second man patted the dust from his vest and pants before going to the door, opening it, and unfolding the stairs. He reached in and started helping the passengers out.

A man exited first, not even sparing Caleb a glance.

A woman with gray hair followed.

Two more men appeared, causing panic to swell in Caleb's chest. Had he been wrong about his bride?

He was about to surrender and admit defeat when a slender, white hand reached out for assistance.

Holding his breath, he watched the woman descend the stairs. She was a little bit of a thing. Young. Too thin. Dressed like a school marm. Her gaze darted around as though searching for someone waiting for her arrival.

"It's her," he whispered, stepping forward to claim his new wife.

As soon as the stagecoach assistant let go of her, Caleb was there, holding out his hand. "Welcome to White Pines. I'm so glad you came."

Tilting her head, she considered him with blue eyes the color of cornflowers. "Thank you."

"You're gonna love it here."

"You knew I was coming?" she asked, her voice a sweet sound to his ears. She clutched a carpetbag handle with one hand while she pushed her black-brown braid back over her shoulder with the other.

Caleb nodded. "The letter—"

"You know about the letter?" Her surprised tone and trembling hand made him want to ease her worries.

"Yes, ma'am. I surely do. I was the one who wanted you to come here. The letter was on my behalf."

"I'm afraid I don't understand."

Feeling foolish, he started to drop his hand.

She stopped him by grasping it tightly. "I don't mean to be rude, sir. I'm grateful for your aid. I just expected..." Giving her head a shake, she let her gaze meet his. "It's kind of you to meet the stage. Will you be taking me to—"

"The church? Oh, yes, ma'am. I ain't gonna compromise your reputation. We're gonna get married proper before I take you out to my farm. I want a wife. A *real* wife—not some doxy to warm my bed." Damn if his cheeks didn't heat to a blush. "If you'll pardon my gutter talk."

"You–you think we're going to marry?" Her eyes were wide with fear, like a doe first scenting danger. "That's why I was asked to come here?"

"Yes, ma'am. A marriage. Good and proper." Crooking his elbow, he placed her hand there, trying to show he had good manners. "I can fetch your baggage, then—"

She dropped her chin and nibbled on her bottom lip. "I fear I have nothing other than my bag. My exit was...hasty."

"None at all?"

With a shake of her head, she tried to ease her hand away. "I understand if you don't wish to follow through with your promise of marriage. It wasn't what I expected anyway. I simply needed a place to stay and a job to earn my keep."

Caleb put his hand over hers, keeping it cradled against his elbow. "It don't matter to me you ain't got much. That ain't why I sent for you. I've got plenty for us both. Please don't fret. I'll take good care of you. I promise. I'll be a good husband in every way. You ain't gonna have to work, except to help out on the farm. I don't even care if you can't cook. I'll teach you."

Her eyes found his again. The pain there tore at his heart, and the shadow of a faded bruise around her right eye explained her timidity. "I'm not...pure. You shouldn't even be thinking of marriage with the likes of me."

So that explained why she'd accepted his bargain. Some man had taken advantage of her, taken her virginity, making her feel as though she'd never make a good marriage.

He'd expected as much, even wondering if the woman who came to him might have a child or two clinging to her skirts. Between the way she'd been compromised and her black eye, she'd been sorely abused.

He could offer her a better life—a solid reason to marry with him. "Don't matter to me none. You're young. Strong. You'll make a good wife, even if you ain't a vir— Um...pure."

Those blue eyes held him captive. He hadn't expected someone so damned pretty. "You'd still have me?" she asked, her voice ragged.

"Yes, ma'am. I surely would."

"I–I don't even know your name."

"Well, now... We can fix that problem right quick. I'm Caleb. Caleb Young. I sent for you with honorable intentions. There just ain't no young women here, and I... To be honest, I'm lonely."

"I'm Sara. Sara Fuller."

Sara. Such a pretty name. Such a pretty face. Even if they'd met under the most proper of circumstances—a church social or a town dance—he'd still have chosen her to court. She was everything he'd ever dreamed of. Didn't matter that she was a mail-order bride.

He couldn't let her get away.

"Then let's go, Sara Fuller. We're going to the church to change your name to Sara Young."

Chapter Two

Sara stood before the preacher, staring at Caleb Young.

My, but he was a handsome devil. Hair and eyes dark as sin. A dimple in his left cheek whenever he smiled. Strong arms that clearly knew hard work.

What was he doing marrying a woman like her?

She wanted to blurt out the myriad questions running through her thoughts. How had her brother arranged this marvel? What had Ty promised him if he took her to wife? Why hadn't Ty told her about his plans to marry her off in his letter, where he'd begged her to leave Denver and come to White Pines?

Then again, her brother had told her this was the perfect place to start over. Perhaps he'd taken it upon himself to find her a husband and a home so she wouldn't be a burden to him and his new wife. That would be very much like Ty—trying to solve every problem.

When she'd stepped off the stagecoach, Caleb had been waiting for her. That, in and of itself, was miraculous. She hadn't written Ty that she was coming, fearing that Crazy Kate would somehow intercept the letter and stop her.

So how had Caleb known she'd be coming on that particular stage?

"Sara? Sweetheart?" Caleb's voice was tender. Kind. "Reverend David is waitin' for your answer." He gave her hands a squeeze.

Her face flushed hot at being caught daydreaming at her own wedding. "I–I'm sorry I... Could you please repeat...?"

She sounded like a ninny.

The preacher gave her a sympathetic smile. The gray-haired man had probably dealt with many a nervous bride. "Will you accept Caleb as your husband?"

Although she'd been honest with Caleb—at least as honest as she could be on a public street—he'd insisted he still wanted her for his wife. The guilt at not telling him the whole truth was easily swept aside. Life had treated her poorly. If this man was willing to marry her, she wasn't about to walk away from that miracle.

Ty had surely told Caleb about her past. There was no way her brother would trap someone into marrying a whore. Ty was too honest to do something so reprehensible.

Caleb was sure to expect husbandly rights. But she'd be giving herself to only one man, not anyone who could put money in Crazy Kate's hand. She'd have a home of her own. She was smart. Surely she'd be able to learn to cook and clean and take care of him.

Just him.

Perhaps one day, she might even learn to like the act of mating.

Perhaps one day it wouldn't bring pain and shame.

Would she take this man as her husband? "I will."

Caleb repeated his own promise to honor and protect her in a clear and steady voice, making Sara wince in her mind. He couldn't know what he was doing. This all had to be a mistake. There was no way on God's green earth that Ty had sent him to her.

Was there?

She was so very tired. All she wanted was to rest—*really* rest. To know peace after watching her back and living in fear and abuse for so long.

"I now pronounce you man and wi—"

"Stop!"

A tall man with hair the same raven shade as Caleb's came striding up the aisle of the small church, head down like an enraged bull.

Sara instinctively stepped in front of Caleb to protect him the same way she had any new girl forced to work at The Palace whenever a customer got mean.

Caleb grabbed her waist and stepped to her side. "Sara, what are you—"

"Stop this damn wedding!" The man stopped in front of the couple and scowled down at her.

"Gideon…" Caleb snaked an arm around her waist and hauled her up against his side, "this is my wife, Sara." He smiled at her, a genuine smile. "Sara, this is my brother, Gideon."

"She ain't your wife yet," Gideon insisted.

The preacher cleared his throat and closed his black book. "I'm afraid you're wrong, Gideon. I just united them in marriage."

"Then *un*-unite 'em." While Caleb's brown eyes were full of compassion, Gideon's burned with anger as he continued to frown at her. "Who the hell *are* you?"

Caleb pushed her behind his back. "Let it be, brother. She's my wife now. What's done is done. Shouting at her won't change anything."

Since she'd never had a man protect her before, she could only gape at her new husband's back. He was a tall drink of water. Her head barely reached his shoulders, and she had to stand on tiptoes to look over him at Gideon. While she was glad to know he was family and probably not a danger, she wasn't about to let her guard down.

He was even taller than Caleb, and his disposition seemed surly. "You don't know nothing about her," Gideon insisted. "You can't marry a stranger."

"I already did," Caleb calmly replied.

"You've yet to kiss your bride," the preacher said with a lopsided smile.

Caleb dismissed his brother by turning his back. Without a word, he wrapped his arms around her and kissed her.

The kiss was over and done before she could react. She stood there, dumbfounded at a kiss that was nothing like the slobbering kisses her customers had offered—one of the reasons she'd avoided kissing as much as she could. This one was warm and sent a shiver of pleasure racing through her.

Gideon had set his fists against his hips and was trying to glare her into submission.

Sara raised her chin and straightened her spine, glad the pride she'd feared was lost had kicked back in.

Caleb fished some money from his pocket, handed it to the preacher, and murmured his appreciation.

After accepting the funds, the preacher left through a side door, probably wanting to let the brothers talk through their differences in private.

Caleb took Sara's hand and picked up her bag. "Ready to go see your new home?"

Gideon's anger shifted its target. "Don't you *dare* take her to your house. How do you know she ain't gonna rob you blind or kill you in your own bed?"

Letting go of her hand and dropping the heavy bag to the floor, Caleb stepped forward to stand toe-to-toe with his brother. "She's my wife now. Accept that. Please, Gideon. Accept *my* choice for *my* life. You ain't changing what's already done."

The tension in the air grew as the brothers continued to stare at each other. Sara knew neither of them well, but she owed her loyalty to her new husband. Ty wouldn't have chosen someone weak to marry her, and she tried not to worry that the Young brothers would come to blows over her. Both were clenching and unclenching their hands and breathing hard enough their nostrils flared.

As more long moments passed, she decided to try to bring a peaceful conclusion to the confrontation. She stepped to Caleb's side and took one of his fisted hands in hers. "I'll try to make you a good wife."

Caleb's gaze caught hers, and the anger ebbed as his dark eyes softened. He relaxed his hand and threaded his fingers through hers. "I know you will."

With a nod, she shifted her attention to Gideon. "I came here to make a new life. I'll try my best to help Caleb run his farm. I'll also try my best to be a good wife to him. I truly want to make this work—for all of us."

She meant every word. This gift—this *blessing*—was her new start. The past could be left behind, and she no longer had to live a life full of violence and degradation.

Sara felt reborn.

All she had to do to begin her new life was convince Caleb's brother of her sincerity.

"I mean what I say, Gideon," Sara said, her voice as full of confidence as she could manage. "Montana is a new start for me."

"And this marriage," Caleb added, "is a new start for me."

Gideon ran his hand over his face and looked away. With a sigh, he dropped his hands to his sides. Without another word, he turned on his heel and marched out of the church.

After the door slammed shut, Caleb leaned in to brush a kiss over her cheek. "Thank you, Sara."

"Why are you thanking me?"

"For the promises you just made to my brother. He'll come around. Just give him some time. Drew will get him to accept you."

"Drew? You have another brother?" She had so much to learn about her new husband and his life. Her only hope was that a new brother—and the rest of Caleb's family—wouldn't be as dead set against her as Gideon was.

Caleb rubbed the back of his neck, clearly frustrated. "Sara.... Drew is Gideon's...um... special friend."

She cocked her head. "Special friend?"

"Drew and Gideon are...close. They...um...live together in his new house near the southern property line, farther from town."

The truth came on her suddenly. There were a few young men working for Crazy Kate. "Oh... Oh, I think I understand." Although her cheeks flushed, she pressed on. "Some men prefer the company of other men rather than women. Is that what you're telling me? That Gideon and Drew are those kind of men?"

He gave her a brusque nod.

Grateful he didn't ask how she'd gathered her knowledge of men's sexual habits, she smiled and chose another subject. "How far is your farm?"

"Our farm."

Her smile broadened. A home. Her whole life that was all she'd ever wanted. Her own home. "Our farm," she said in a breathless whisper. Suddenly anxious to get her new future started, she couldn't help but ask, "Is it close to town?"

He nodded. "Only about an hour's drive." Tugging her along with him, he headed toward the door. "Are you ready to go home, Mrs. Young?"

"Mrs. Young." As all that had happened began to settle on her, she wanted to twirl around and shout her happiness. "I like the sound of that."

***

The ride back to his farm passed in silence. Caleb had so much he wanted to tell Sara, so much more he wanted to ask. He simply couldn't get his mind off the fact this was his wedding night. He had a beautiful bride, and he wasn't sure how to approach the topic of consummating the marriage.

Sara seemed to enjoy the quiet, and he needed the time to formulate a plan. While he might've told people he'd sought a wife to share the work at the farm and to spend time with, truth was he wanted intimacy most of all.

He knew a few whores who'd set up shop nearby. They kept to themselves, having customers visit them in their cabin just outside White Pines. No one thought poorly of them, and married men gave them wide berth. Their visitors were mostly cowboys and single men—like Caleb—who were doing nothing more than easing the demands of their bodies.

While he'd found the physical release he so desperately needed in that cabin, he couldn't ignore that he was sinning. Each and every visit might have slaked his lust, but he was left with a troubled conscience and a feeling of shame. Most times the need struck him he simply took matters into his own hands.

But now he had a wife—a sweet and pretty young woman who he hoped would learn to love the marriage bed.

Caleb found himself with a problem he hadn't anticipated. Sara had been abused. She might not have told him in so many words, but the yellowed, fading bruise around her right eye and the way her voice had trembled when she'd admitted she wasn't a virgin shouted the fact. He'd have to coax her into making love.

The thought that she might not be ready for intimacy brought a groan.

Sara turned to look at him, her eyes sparkling in the fading sunlight. "Are you ill?"

"No. No, just...thinking."

"It must've been an uncomfortable thought."

Since his cock was already hard in anticipation of making love to her, he chuckled. "Yeah...*very* uncomfortable." He shifted in his seat, although it did little to help his predicament.

He wanted her, and not because she was a female. She was a

sweet-tempered woman, and he enjoyed the spark of courage he'd witnessed when she'd pushed him behind her to protect him from Gideon. She was a beauty, too. And although a bit cautious, guarding her words, he'd seen a streak of humor in her.

No, Sara was more than a simple woman. She was his wife, and he already felt a possessiveness that startled him with its intensity.

"Gettin' close," he said, pointing to the last turn. "The house is on that road."

She bounced on her seat, her excitement palpable. "Is it large? Not that I need a big home, mind you. I'm simply curious."

"Yes, ma'am, it's large. Three whole bedrooms. It was my parents' home before they passed on. Then Gideon and me took it over."

"You lost your parents?"

Caleb nodded. "The flu swept the town ten years back. Took a good share of the population, including my sister and my parents."

She picked up his hand and cradled it in hers. "I'm so sorry. You must've been so young..."

"Yes, ma'am. I was only thirteen. Gideon was twenty-two. He raised me after that. That's why he was so upset. He still thinks he needs to protect me."

"From me." Although she held tight to his hand, she glanced away. "He doesn't approve of you marrying me."

Giving her hand a squeeze, he hoped to ease her worries. "It weren't you, Sara. He didn't want me to marry this way. That's all."

"This way? You mean having the marriage arranged?"

"Yes, ma'am."

"Caleb?"

"Yes?"

"I think you can stop calling me 'ma'am.' I'm your wife now."

"Yes, ma— Sara. Yes, Sara."

God, he loved her smile.

The wagon shifted through the ruts on the road, forcing Sara to slide closer to him. Their thighs brushed, sending heat blazing straight to his groin. This time, he swallowed his groan.

She didn't move away, and he liked that she still held tight to his hand.

Caleb didn't let go until he had to ease the horses' pace as they pulled up to his home. "We're here."

"Oh...my..." Her gaze wandered the house. "It *is* big. How many rooms?"

"Six."

"Six?"

"Yes, ma— Yes, Sara. And I even have a bathroom. Tub and all."

Her eyes widened. "A real bathroom?"

He nodded.

Her gaze dropped to her lap as she smoothed her hands over her skirt. "My clothes are covered in filth, and I imagine I smell as rank as your manure pile."

"You do no such thing."

"May I have a bath? Please?"

Climbing down, Caleb reached up to lift Sara from the wagon. Instead of releasing her, he held tight to her waist and stared down into her eyes. "Yes. You may have a bath."

Her smile took his breath away. "Thank you."

"You don't have to thank me. This is your home now."

"Truly?"

Why would she doubt him? He'd gone to great trouble and expense to bring her all the way from St. Louis. Surely she knew he wouldn't go to such lengths if he hadn't intended on sharing his life with her.

Time, he reminded himself. Sara would need time to get over her abusive past.

"Truly," he replied.

And still, he wouldn't release her. Having her close seemed so right, and he tightened his grip, pulling her even closer until her breasts brushed his chest.

Caleb sucked in a hissing breath.

Sara's eyes widened before her lids dropped to half mast, looking drowsy and downright sexy.

He had to kiss her. From the moment his lips had touched hers after the ceremony, he'd wanted to taste her fully. Going slow, giving her time to pull away, he lowered his head to hers.

Sara had been dying to see if the wedding kiss was some odd occurrence or if Caleb's kiss was really different from those she'd received from greedy customers. She rose on her toes to meet him halfway.

When his lips touched hers, she felt the same shiver racing the length of her spine. The kiss was gentle, his lips firm and yet soft. Ever so slowly, he increased the pressure, letting her know there was hunger behind the kiss.

He tasted like...*more.*

She fisted her hands in his jacket and tickled his lips with her tongue. When he opened them to her, she slid her tongue into his mouth.

His demeanor changed as he wrapped his arms around her and embraced her with a ferocity that left her breathless. The kiss became wild as his tongue chased hers into her mouth. One hand grasped her braid while his other settled on her backside, pulling her hard against him.

The moment his erection rubbed against her lower belly, her whole body stiffened in response.

It was instinctual, the fear of a hardened cock. Sara had loved Caleb's kisses, wanting to surrender to whatever magic had held her in its grasp. That magic had ended when the reality of her situation hit.

Caleb wanted sex.

Exactly what every man in her life had ever wanted from her.

Caleb eased his grip. "It's okay, Sara. I understand. I'll be gentle with you. I promise."

How many times had she heard that same promise from a man only moments before he gave her pain?

She glanced away, surrendering to the inevitable. She'd known all along that this dream couldn't possibly last. One day—or night, rather—she'd have to awaken to stark reality. Her new husband was no different than any other man.

"I know," she said with a resigned sigh.

His crooked finger lifted her chin until she was staring into his eyes again. "No, you don't. You don't know me at all, short of having stood before a preacher and sayin' our vows."

"It's okay, Caleb. You're a man. I–I understand what you want."

"I do want you. I admit that freely. But I'll be gentle."

He swept her into his arms and carried her into the house.

Chapter Three

When Caleb released her, Sara was unsteady on her feet. The darkness made her disoriented, so she stood patiently while Caleb set her bag aside and lit the lamps.

The home wasn't the log cabin she'd pictured as a Montana homestead.

They were in a large parlor—much larger than she would've expected after seeing the house from the outside. The darkness had obviously concealed its true size.

As light cast all around, she marveled at the furnishings. The floor was smooth wood, and although there was no carpet, the shine of the polished surface in the lamplight was inviting. Two beautifully carved rocking chairs sat on either side of the pot-bellied stove. Their twisted spindles had to have taken hours upon hours to create. She ran her fingers over the back of one chair, touching the roses in full bloom that had been etched into the wood.

A large set of shelves was topped with a carved image of a horse in full gallop, his mane and tail had been delicately engraved. On the shelves sat two worn books and statues of Indians and animals ranging from deer to raccoons.

She picked up one of the carvings and considered it more closely. Not a dog as she'd first supposed but a wolf. "This is beautiful. So detailed. So lifelike." Tracing the ridges of the fur, she glanced to her new husband. "Did you make this?"

His cheeks were stained with a blush. "Yes, ma'am."

"You made all of these?"

"Yes, ma— Sara. Gets mighty lonely since Gideon moved away."

Her sympathy went out to him, and for a moment, her battered heart allowed her to see a child—a child she should've shared with Caleb—playing with the wolf.

Then she sobered.

Sara could never bear a child. Her husband would surely be disappointed, but she hadn't found the courage to tell him before they'd exchanged vows. If he'd known, he would have stopped the wedding.

And then where would she be?

He'd made no mention of wanting a family, only a wife. She would have to be enough for him thanks to Crazy Kate.

The memories still burned like the hottest fire. Sara had barely realized she was expecting when Kate had her drugged with laudanum and tied to a bed while a man tore her child from her womb with dirty surgical instruments. After suffering through weeks of fevers and bleeding, she'd recovered. But she'd never conceived again, leaving her convinced she was barren.

Sara set the wolf and any dreams of having a family aside. She shed her coat, looking around for a place to hang it.

Caleb came to her rescue, taking it from her and hanging it on a coat tree she'd missed. After he took off his own coat, he hung it up as well. "What do you think?"

"Of the house?"

He nodded.

"It's lovely. So much more than I ever would've dreamed. I feel blessed to be able to call it home now."

His grin told her that her words had pleased him.

As he took a step closer, his eyes darkening in what she recognized as desire, she held out her hand to stop him. She couldn't stop the inevitable—the consummation of the marriage—nor did she want to. The legality of their union could be questioned if there wasn't a proper bedding. Although she dreaded it, she was resigned to the reality that she wanted this marriage to last and would do anything she could to ensure it did.

"I–I would like to bathe first," Sara said.

Caleb watched her warily.

"We can...be together after," she reminded him. "I wish to be clean and have a clean nightgown."

He glanced at the carpetbag. "You ain't got a nightgown?"

"I didn't have time... I couldn't...um..." Couldn't what? Bring anything with her?

Even if she'd wanted to, all of her old clothes would be entirely unsuitable for polite folk—nothing but gaudy beads, tattered lace, and wilted feathers. The outfit she wore now was all she owned that was respectable, and she'd kept it carefully hidden until she could save enough money to run away. She'd folded the skirt, shirt, and coat into a tight bundle and laid it below loose floorboards in her room at the cathouse. Every time Kate strode across the room, the boards had squeaked, the sound terrifying Sara—yet it also emboldened her, reminding her of her plan to escape.

"I have some money," she said. "If we could go back into town tomorrow, I could purchase some clothing."

"Actually..." Caleb strode to a large trunk sitting below a cross with a carved image of Jesus hanging upon it. "I have all of my mother's things." He knelt and opened the trunk's lid. "She was a little bit of thing," he said over his shoulder. "Just like you."

"I couldn't possibly wear your mother's clothes." The thought was horrifying, probably because Sara wasn't the type of woman his mother would've chosen for his bride. Heavens, she wasn't the kind of woman *any* mother would want for her well-reared, God-fearing son.

Tears burned her eyes, but she refused to let a single one fall no matter how much guilt pressed down on her. She'd trapped this man—this sweet, kind, wonderful man. Her brother might have arranged this match, but she'd agreed. She'd stood before the preacher and spoken vows binding her to Caleb Young for the rest of her days.

What's done is done. Let it be, Sara.

Caleb lifted a folded garment from the trunk and shut the lid. He strode over to her and held it out. "This nightgown should work for now. You can go through the rest of Ma's things tomorrow to see what will work. Or we could go into town. I could buy you some new things, if you'd prefer."

Sara hesitated, almost afraid to touch the snow white fabric as though her touch would taint it.

Stop it. You're not a bad woman. You're not!

The things she'd done had been necessary to survive. She was strong. She could put this behind her and make a new life, just as she'd planned. The difference was that the new life now included Caleb.

"Please, Sara. Take it. I'd be pleased that you'll have somethin' comfy to wear while you sleep." He gave her the gown and led her to another door. Opening it, he nodded at the interior. "A real bath. Tub and all. Mighty proud of that."

"As you should be."

He followed her into the bathroom.

"I'm going to bathe," she reminded him.

"And I'm going to help." Taking the nightgown back, he set it aside.

Sara tried not to tremble as he slowly unbuttoned her shirt. One skill she'd learned early in her time at The Palace was to size up a man, to know whether he was going to be kind or cruel. Caleb would be gentle with her, and she had nothing to fear.

But she also had nothing to enjoy.

That's not true, you silly girl.

There was much to enjoy about this new life. A beautiful home—much grander than she'd ever lived in. A chance to be with just one man—a clean, considerate man. And a chance to dig deep and perhaps one day regain her self-respect by being a good wife.

Surrendering to him, Sara slid her feet out of her shoes and stared up at her new husband.

Caleb opened her shirt, tugging it from the waistband of her skirt and then easing it off her shoulders. It fell to the floor, and he stared at her breasts as they swelled above her corset.

Her camisole was badly worn, having been mended more times

than she could remember. The threadbare fabric did little to hide her nipples, which had hardened in the chill air. The silence between husband and wife stretched as he continued to stare and she feared he didn't like what he saw.

She was too thin, something Crazy Kate had scolded her for again and again. Although there was plenty to eat—and drink—at The Palace, Sara had little appetite. Because she was so finicky about her food, she was lithe. Her breasts weren't nearly as full as any of the other girls. A buxom bunch, most on the plump side with the rounded hips and cherubic shapes the men seemed to prefer.

She worried Caleb would think her less than womanly because of her small breasts and lean body.

He unfastened the buttons on the side of her skirt. With a low growl, he tugged it down. The material puddled at her feet.

She wasn't wearing a petticoat, only a pair of worn pantalets with ragged lace edging.

"Damn." His gaze swept her figure. "God, I'm a lucky man," he said in a breathless whisper as he jerked at the corset's fasteners, freeing her from the tight garment. His head bowed, and he licked a nipple through the camisole.

The same tingle of delight she'd experienced with his kiss raced through her, a feeling both foreign and frightening. Some of the girls loved mating. Their cries of delight often rang through the paper-thin walls. She'd never understood that. Sex for her was an act that completed a financial transaction. Most of the time, she simply tolerated it. Other times, it caused her pain. Every time, she was beyond glad when it was over.

Since the desire was still clear in his eyes—that, and his breathing had grown rough and ragged—she was assured he wasn't disappointed. He knelt in front of her, untying her garters and tossing those ribbons over his shoulder. His fingers brushed against the skin of her thigh as he peeled down her stockings.

She closed her eyes. Her bath was going to have to wait.

All Caleb could do was gape at the beauty before him. Never in his wildest dreams could he have imagined he'd be married to an angel like Sara.

Now she stood before him in undergarments that revealed more than they hid, and he wanted her so badly, he knew they'd never even make it to the bed.

He jerked his own shirt open, letting the buttons fall like hailstones on the wooden floor. In his haste, he didn't realize his boots were still on until his pants got all tangled up and he nearly pitched forward at his new bride.

A blush heating his cheeks, he fumbled to remove all of his clothes, casting them aside and then hurrying back to pull Sara into his arms.

The feel of her against him enflamed his yearning. He wanted to know all of her, to possess all of her. His mouth came down on hers, hard and urgent. His control had vanished, and he kissed her with a ferocity that surprised him—and yet he couldn't gentle the kiss. He needed her surrender, demanded it by forcing his tongue into her mouth. Her taste was intoxicating, and he learned it, memorized it, savored it.

She tried to turn her head. Caleb wouldn't allow it, holding her tighter against him as his tongue explored her mouth. Although she was holding back, she wasn't fighting the kiss. After long moments, her tongue finally rubbed across his, forcing another growl to rumble deep in his chest.

He broke away, gasping for air as he pulled her camisole over her head and then untied her pantalets. Shoving them over her hips, he grabbed a drying cloth from where it laid draped over the side of the tub and spread it over the pile of their discarded clothing. Then he picked her up and set her on it, dropping down beside her.

Caleb was wild now, barely able to temper any of his actions. He wanted Sara to like it, but his thoughts were lost in the unquenched desire that had been eating him alive for so very long. As he smoothed his hand over her flat stomach, he leaned down and drew one of her puckered nipples into his mouth. He suckled while he let his fingers comb through the dark hair on her mound and then slide between her folds.

Trying to coax her response was more than he could handle. He knew little of a woman's body, having heard some women simply couldn't enjoy bed sports. Sara made little moans and sighs, but something about her reactions niggled in his thoughts. Sinking a finger deep inside her, he lost the last of his ability to think at all.

"I can't wait, Sara," he mumbled as he spread her thighs with his knee and settled his cock against her sheath.

Lost in need, he plunged into her. Again and again he thrust into her tight heat, feeling his release building inside him until he thought he'd explode.

Caleb spilled his seed into Sara with a shout of surrender before collapsing on her, trying to shield her from some of his weight by holding himself up on his elbows. His heartbeat thundered in his ears, and his eyes were closed tight. Moments passed in an awkward quiet as he tried to grab hold of his tumbling thoughts.

His body was sated, and he should've felt some contentment for having made love to his new bride.

Ah, but there was the problem. He'd been so lost in his own need, he hadn't taken care to make sure Sara enjoyed the loving as well.

Opening his eyes, he pushed himself up enough he could look at her face. What he saw there was almost enough to make him weep in shame.

Her eyes were slumberous, almost as though she was about to drift off to sleep. There was no flush on her cheeks, no signs at all that she'd enjoyed their interlude. She hadn't wrapped her legs around his hips or scored her nails across his back—nothing to show she'd even been an active participant.

All of his contentment vanished.

What had happened between them was no different than the visits he'd made to the cabin outside of town. The whores there had treated him much the same. They'd tried to stroke his masculine ego with fake sounds of pleasure, but he'd known the truth. They'd tolerated his use of their body.

The same way Sara just had.

"May I bathe now?" she asked, pushing against his chest.

Caleb rolled away. "That was selfish of me."

She didn't reply, only stood, jerked up the drying cloth, and immediately wrapped it around her body.

He grabbed her wrist when she tried to step away. "I mean it, Sara. That was selfish of me. I'm sorry."

Her gaze found his, and he hated the sadness reflected in her eyes. "You have nothing to be sorry for, Caleb. I'm your wife now. I know my duty."

"I was too...needy. I was too rough with you."

"You were quite gentle," she replied with a shrug.

"I used you," he bluntly said. "That's not how it should be between us. I don't want this to be your...*duty*."

With another delicate shrug, she pulled her wrist free and headed to the tub.

"I should heat the water." Caleb got to his feet, fished out his pants, and donned them. "I'll have your bath ready right away."

It was the least he could do.

***

Sarah found Caleb waiting in the bed.

As soon as her eyes caught his, he pulled the quilt back and patted the spot next to him.

She snuffed out the last lamp and crawled onto the bed, settling herself on her side so she could see him.

He stared back.

Although she was bone-weary, her curiosity was killing her. "I don't understand why you agreed to this marriage."

"Told you. I was lonely."

"Surely there are women here who would thank their lucky stars to have such a handsome husband and a beautiful home like this."

His eyes widened. "You think I'm handsome?"

She saw no reason to play coy. "I do."

He brushed a quick kiss over her mouth. "I think you're damned pretty."

The compliment was welcomed but disbelieved.

"I sent for you," he explained, "'cause there ain't an unmarried woman anywhere in the territory."

"But Montana is…enormous. There have to be—"

He was already shaking his head. "Lots of land, but not lots of folks."

"No other woman captured your heart?"

"No, ma'am…er, Sara. Had a fancy for Cassie Shay when she showed up in town, but then another rascal snatched her up." He followed his word with a wink.

Sara liked the way he teased her about Ty being a "rascal." Ty and Cassie were happily married according to her brother's letter. Besides, had Caleb won Cassie, where would Sara be now?

A yawn slipped out, one she didn't bother hiding behind her hand. "I fear I shall be asleep soon."

Caleb rolled her to her back and rose over her. "You're tuckered out. Get some sleep." He gave her another no-nonsense kiss. Then he flopped to his side and moved her around until she laid on her other side, her back pressed to his chest. He molded the fronts of his thighs to the backs of her, and his erection told her he was going to be a greedy husband.

But that was a blessing. One man. All she would have to tolerate was *one* man.

She fell asleep with a smile on her face.

Caleb couldn't sleep.

Although his body hummed in satisfaction, his thoughts tumbled around and around. He knew little of women, but he did know Sara hadn't enjoyed their lovemaking.

Not that he'd been much of a *lover*… All he'd done was take. His body had demanded, and he'd surrendered his control to the lust pounding through him.

Never again, he vowed.

When he took his wife again, she would be a willing, active participant. While he didn't possess much knowledge of how a woman's body worked, he was an eager student. If Sara was willing to teach him what pleased her—and what didn't—they could work together to make their beddings something enjoyable for *both* of them.

Caleb nuzzled her neck, kissing the hollow behind her ear.

Sara let out a sigh and brushed her sweet backside against his groin.

Hell's fire, he wanted her again. Now. His cock hadn't even softened after his climax, but he wasn't about to use his bride again just to slake his lust.

There was more at stake here than he'd realized. While he'd been searching for a wife, he'd naïvely assumed she'd be a biddable, obedient woman. He hadn't considered that she'd have a strong personality or a past that haunted her.

That's what you get for thinking with your cock.

Well, Sara might not have been who he'd bargained for as a wife, but that was exactly who she was. His wife. They'd been legally wed, the marriage consummated, albeit ineptly on his part. His duty was to make her happy. Besides, a biddable, obedient wife might quickly bore him. He liked the fire he saw in Sara, knowing there was more to her than what she'd allowed him to see. He would win her trust so he could break through to find the real woman hiding behind the mask.

Before sleep claimed him, Caleb's last thought was that he was a very lucky man.

Chapter Four

Sara woke, startled to find a man in bed with her.

Kate never let customers spend the night, knowing they'd want a second go. No way she'd lose that kind of profit. A whole night cost a cowboy a week's pay. Few would spend money on the luxury.

Her memories of the day before came slamming back. Caleb Young—her husband—slept at her side, snoring and relaxed as though he didn't have a care in the world.

Easing out of bed, she figured she should make breakfast. She was, after all, a wife now. Problem was she had no idea how to cook anything.

Donning her wrinkled clothes, she hurried to the kitchen. She hadn't had a chance to see it last night. Probably a good thing because Caleb might have wanted her to cook them some supper. Her stomach rumbled its emptiness since she hadn't eaten anything but stale bread and cheese in more than a day.

There was a stove with pots and pans hanging on the wall at its side. She pulled down a frying pan, planning to make some eggs and perhaps ham if she could find some smoked meat. The food at The Palace was prepared for the girls by a Chinese woman, leaving Sara ill-equipped for the task. Since there weren't any eggs to be found, she donned her coat and headed outside to fetch some from the hen house she'd spied when they'd arrived on the farm the night before. After risking her safety to fight with the enraged hens, she was able to retrieve six eggs, only suffering four scratches in the process. A fair trade.

Caleb waited for her at the door, wearing nothing but his pants. His suspenders hung from his hips as he leaned a shoulder against the door frame. He wasn't even shivering from the cold.

"I was worried," he said when she passed by him to go inside.

"Worried?"

He followed her to the kitchen. "I feared you might've...left."

"Why would I leave?"

His response was a shrug as he followed her inside and shut the door. Then he held the eggs as she hung up her coat.

He started a fire in the stove while she cracked the eggs into a large ceramic bowl. Most of the girls at The Palace liked their eggs scrambled, so she would try that and hope for the best.

How difficult could it be to cook a few eggs?

"Fire's going," Caleb said as he stood to brush his hands against his pants.

"Thank you."

"Gonna wash up and finish dressing."

She gave him a nod. "I'll cook breakfast. Then I assume we'll have chores."

He glanced out the window. "We slept pretty late. Might take us some time to catch up. Spent a lot of yesterday waitin' on the stage. Fell a bit behind." Coming up behind her, he ran his palms down her arms as she whipped the eggs with a fork. He kissed her cheek. "I'll show you around the farm after breakfast."

Before Sara could ask him how he knew she'd be on that stage, he was gone.

***

The acrid smell of smoke hit Caleb right after he put on his boots.

"Sara?" The smell grew stronger, making him speed his pace as he raced to the kitchen.

"Caleb! Help!"

He found her trying to slap out the flames in the frying pan with a towel.

Snatching the towel from her hand, he wrapped it around the pan's handle and hurried to the sink. A few hard pumps sent water spewing from the cistern, drowning the fire.

"Hell's fire, woman! What happened?"

"I believe I scorched the eggs."

"Scorched the— You near to set the whole house on fire!"

Striding back toward her, he raked his fingers through his hair.

Sara flinched, causing him to stop his hand in midair.

All of his anger evaporated. "I ain't gonna hit you."

Slowly, she turned back to him. Wariness swam in her eyes.

"I mean it, Sara. I ain't never gonna hit you. Ain't right for a man to strike a lady."

Still, she said nothing, only watched him with her intense blue eyes.

Caleb wanted to demand that she trust him—right here, right now. But trust couldn't be demanded—it had to be earned. That took time. "It's all right now. Fire's out."

"I should clean up," she said as she tried to brush past him.

He stopped her with a hand on her upper arm, then he pulled her closer and set his hands on her waist. The tips of her feet brushed his. With a crooked finger, he lifted her chin until she was looking at him. "I swear to you, Sara. I'll never hurt you."

"Kate always said husbands could beat their wives."

"Who's Kate?"

A moment of panic flashed over her features before a mask of calm settled. "A friend from Denver," she replied in a flat voice.

"A good friend? Would she wanna come out here? There are other men like me who need a wife and—"

To his surprise, Sara's mood changed yet again. This time she shifted into laughter, the amusement reaching her eyes. "I doubt too many men like you would want to take Kate to wife."

"You don't know how to cook, do you?" he asked.

"I fear I don't. But I can learn. I'm a quick study."

Caleb kissed her forehead. "Then I'll have to take you out to Twin Springs."

"Twin Springs?"

"Adam Morgan's ranch. His wife's the best cook in the territory. Grace loves teaching other ladies cooking." Picking up the dirty bowl, he said, "How about I cook for now? Still want eggs?"

"I would be happy with anything," Sara replied.

"Then get your pretty self out to the coop and fetch us a few more eggs while I clean up the skillet. I'll fry us up some eggs and bacon."

***

Sara stood on the bottom board of the stall, leaning over the top board to talk to Caleb as he milked one of his cows. "Doesn't that hurt her?"

With a smile, he just kept squeezing milk from the teats into a bucket. "Don't seem to. Imagine she'd feel worse if I didn't milk her."

"Why?" Everything here was so new, and Sara had a million questions.

"Did you see how full her udder was when I started on her?"

"You mean that big...um...sack?"

"Yep."

"I saw." Understanding dawned. "It's much smaller now." A horrible thought crossed her mind. "Would it explode if you didn't squeeze out the milk?"

His chuckle was warm and his smile held no condescension. "Doubt it. Might hurt her some, but nature would win out. Her milk would dry up."

A glance around the barn yielded more questions. "Why do you only have two cows? Shouldn't you have more if you sell milk?"

"Ain't a dairy farmer." Another chuckle slipped out. "Ain't really a farmer at all."

"Now you're speaking in riddles," Sara scolded.

"I'm sorry, sweetheart." Caleb grabbed the bucket and poured the milk into a large galvanized can except for the small amount he poured into a bowl.

A black cat scrambled from the top of the hay bales, jumping down and padding over to lap at the milk.

Caleb set the bucket aside, went to her, and lifted her off the gate. Keeping his hands on her waist, he turned her to face him.

A shiver of excitement raced through her as he eased forward, the anticipation of the kiss making her lightheaded. She'd never imagined enjoying kissing so much and was glad this was something she could share with her new husband, something not truly tainted by her past.

The kiss was short and sweet and left her with a heated flush deep inside her. This was so new, and she loved the way Caleb made her feel as though there were no pressure for more, that he was giving her a simple sign of his affection.

Of course he didn't truly hold affection for her. He barely even knew her. Perhaps he was only playing the role of a dutiful husband.

It was enough.

Still holding her waist, he stared down at her. "My family's rich."

The man had a talent for keeping her off balance. "I beg your pardon?"

Why his face flamed was a mystery. What did he have to be embarrassed about?

"M–my family is…um…rich. *I'm* rich, Sara. My parents left me and Gideon all their money."

"I'm sorry. I don't understand."

He kissed her forehead and turned her loose. "What's to understand?" Taking her hand, he snatched a bridle off a hook and led her from the barn. He stopped at the small corral where two horses munched contentedly on flakes of hay he'd tossed in earlier.

"If you're wealthy," she asked, "why are you living in the wilderness?"

"Montana ain't really the wilderness nowadays."

Although Sara was convinced Caleb's claim to wealth was a ruse—an amusement to tease her and perhaps learn something about her character—she still couldn't contain her reaction. "B–but you could live in New York or Chicago or even travel the world. You could see London or Paris!"

"Don't wanna go to Paris. Don't wanna go to New York. Montana's my home." He opened the gate as the bay horse came right up to nuzzle his hand. Caleb obliged the animal with a pat. "Ready, Check?"

"His name is Check? As in the game of chess?" Since she'd seen a set of carved pieces on the shelf in the house, she'd assumed he enjoyed the game. Perhaps she could coax him into playing against her. Although it wasn't her favorite way to pass time, it might be something they could share.

"Yes, ma'am." Caleb put the bit in the horse's mouth and fit the bridle around his ears. Then he jumped on its back and held his hand down to her. "Wanna ride around? I can show you our farm."

"I thought you told me it wasn't a farm." Sara wanted to stall long enough for him to give up the idea. "How did you parents earn their wealth?"

She was sure he hadn't seen her relief that he'd taken her home in a wagon rather than on horseback. Living in Denver, she'd been able to avoid any chance at having to ride. But Montana was her home now, and she'd need to ride. Somehow she'd have to conquer her fear.

"They got lucky in the gold fields," he replied. "This is a small farm. Just big enough to feed us without relying on the other folks. That's what my parents wanted. A place of their own well away from the craziness of California." He leaned down closer, again offering his hand. "I'd love to show you everything."

The panic in his new wife's eyes as she backed away from his outstretched hand made Caleb slide off Check's back and go to her. "Sara? Honey? What's—"

"I can't." Shaking her head, she stumbled back a few more steps. "Please don't make me."

The way she kept moving away from him made him frown and follow. He caught her hand and then gathered her into his arms. Holding her tight, he rested his cheek on top of her head and waited for her to stop trembling.

"Why didn't you tell me you were a'feared of horses?"

"I'm not."

"Then why—"

"I mean I'm not afraid of the animals themselves. I'm afraid of riding them."

Caleb stroked her hair, enjoying the way her appealing scent filled his senses. "You don't have to ride."

Sara eased back to glance up at him. "I'm being silly, I know. I just fear riding—especially on a horse as big as Check."

Although Check was pretty average as horses went, Caleb didn't have the heart to contradict her. Instead, he let Sara go and stripped the bridle from his horse. A pat on the rump sent Check trotting back into the paddock.

Nodding at the white mare who hurried up to eat the flake of hay Caleb tossed over the fence, Sara asked, "What's the white's name?"

"She's Mate."

At least Sara chuckled at the pun he'd intended when he'd named the horses. "Clever, clever Caleb."

"I mean it, Sara. You don't have to ride if you don't want to." His gaze captured hers, and although he understood the wariness in her expression, he wished he could end it by earning her trust. "You don't have to do *anything* you don't want to."

She dropped her chin.

He framed her cheeks in his hands and made her look at him. "I won't bed you again 'til you're ready."

"I'm ready."

"You ain't," he insisted. "I know you didn't enjoy it last night."

A bright brush spread over her cheeks. "Must we talk of this?"

"We must. The loving is an important part of marriage. I want to please you as much as you pleased me."

"It was fine, Caleb. Truly it was."

"Promise me something?"

"Anything."

He stroked her cheeks with his thumbs, pleased with her quick response. "Promise me you won't lie to me. Ever. I'll make you the same pledge. Right here. Right now. I'll never lie to you, wife."

Her teeth tugged on her bottom lip.

Caleb was willing to wait while she thought it over. This marriage could work if they both gave it their very best. But if they couldn't be honest with each other from the beginning, the foundation might not be strong enough to endure the hardships and trials life was sure to throw their way.

After a few more moments, Sara gave him her reply. "I promise, husband. I won't lie to you."

"Then tell me what was wrong last night."

"Must I?"

"You must. I need to know, sweetheart. I need to learn what pleases you. I want you to enjoy when we love each other."

A small snort slipped out.

"You doubt my sincerity?" he asked.

"No. No, I believe you're sincere. What I doubt is...me."

There were so many questions he had. While he wanted to ask them all and clear the air, now was not the time to expect her to reveal everything about her past. So he swallowed his curiosity and focused on easing her mind. "I don't doubt you. If you're willing to try—to tell me what you like and–and what you don't—"

"Caleb—"

"No, I mean it. I won't bed you again until I know you're willin' and—"

"I *am* willing."

"*And*," he continued, "until you want me as badly as I want you."

Chapter Five

Sarah sat in one of the wooden chairs, enjoying the heat radiating from the stove.

Winter would be on them soon, and from the stories she'd heard, Montana would be very cold and very snowy. She best get used to it. But for now, she was warm and cozy in her new home.

She set the sewing supplies on her lap and then turned the bodice of the calico dress inside out so she could take in the waist. Caleb was correct—his mother had been a "little bit of a thing." Even so, Sara was smaller.

"What was her name?" Sara asked when Caleb sat in the other chair.

He had a fresh block of wood a little larger than his hand and a small carving knife. "Eleanor."

"What was she like?"

His smile made her happy. "Tough as old jerky but a heart as wide as this territory." The smile grew. "Ma was stubborn. Probably where I get it from."

"I fear we share that trait." She finished threading her needle and started stitching. "I've been told on many, many occasions that I'm more stubborn than should ever be allowed by God. I shall try to keep myself from being too contrary."

"Me, too." Small slivers fell steadily from his efforts with the wood. The scent of pine wafted her way. "You talk good—like you got a good education. Ma and Pa had plenty of money, but Pa didn't cotton to school learning. Always said life could teach me and Gideon a helluva lot more. But you went to school. I can tell."

"I wasn't truly educated, but I paid sharp attention to my companion's tutor."

His hand stilled as he stared at her. "What d'ya mean companion?"

Caleb was right—the only way to make this marriage work was to be honest with each other. She saw no harm in telling him the story of her childhood. After all, her life hadn't been *all* bad. "I was taken in at age five by a wealthy family to serve as a companion for their only child—a daughter of the same age."

"Couldn't they just have another kid?" he asked, shaving another piece off his block of wood.

Sara pricked her finger, making her stop sewing as she told her story. "Jacqueline—my companion—came along after the Colberts were told they would never have children. Mrs. Colbert had a very difficult birth. Jacqueline was...damaged. She couldn't use her legs and was confined to a wheelchair. Her parents were afraid other children wouldn't accept her. So they acquired me."

"Acquired? Makes it sound like they bought you."

In a way, they had. The orphanage sure hadn't been particular about what the Colberts would do with her when she left with them. Sara's memories were of the woman in charge all but sweeping them out the door as she'd mumbled, "One less mouth to feed."

But it was her parents' fault she'd been at the orphanage to begin with.

While Caleb might never meet her blood kin, she couldn't be sure. He already knew Ty, and with her wealth of siblings, they could cross paths. Sara took a diplomatic tack. "They found me in an orphanage and gave me a place to live."

"What happened to your folks? Were they dead?"

"No. They only died a few years ago." Something Ty had told her about when he'd visited her in Denver.

"That don't make no sense." He stopped carving and knit his brows. "They were still alive but took you to an orphanage?"

"It's...complicated." She returned her focus to her sewing, knotting her thread and biting off the excess as she planned how to explain so that she didn't earn her new husband's pity. "My parents were very poor. I was their eighth child. No sooner was I born when my mother found herself with child again. There were simply too many mouths to feed."

"Your pa should've learned a few tricks to keep from making your ma pregnant all the time."

"I agree, but from what my brother told me they were always a bit...reckless. My younger sister and I were placed in a home for girls around my second birthday, about the same time two of my brothers were placed in a different foundling home. The rest were old enough to earn some coin. The Colberts chose me a few years later. I honestly don't remember much from those times. My memories are mostly of being Jacqueline's companion."

Returning to his hobby, Caleb asked, "Why didn't they just adopt you and make you her sister?"

Sara shrugged. "I presume they were blood proud. They were French, you see, and had ties to the former royal family. Or so they claimed..." She'd always doubted those assertions. The Colberts simply didn't believe any child was as important as their miraculous Jacqueline.

"So what does a companion do?"

"Many, many things. I helped her dress and attended to her personal needs. I read to her and kept her entertained. I slept in a cot near Jacqueline's bed in case she was afraid or lonely in the night.

Often I would help change linens should she have an...um...accident. I would bathe and change her and then fix her bedding."

"Change the linens? Are you sure you were a *companion?* Makes you sound like a *servant.*"

Busy with her sewing and discussing a safe topic, Sara let her guard down and allowed the memories to flow. "I suppose I was, but I was content. I was able to go everywhere Jacqueline went. Her tutor liked me and taught me, despite the Colberts telling him he'd receive no pay for my instruction. In fact, they discouraged it for it took my time—and his—away from Jacqueline."

The loud snort and the way he practically stabbed at the wood told her Caleb wasn't enjoying her story. That hinted that he was already becoming attached to her and was offended on her behalf.

That seemed a good sign.

"It was fine, Caleb. Truly it was. I would never have had as fine an education had I not been Jacqueline's companion."

"What else did you do?"

"Whenever we were out and about I kept other children away."

"Why? I'd think they'd want their little girl to play with other children."

That question required some thought. Sara had known her job—to keep Jacqueline safe. She just never pondered the rationale behind the task. "I believe her parents were afraid."

"Afraid?"

"That other children might make her ill or perhaps injure her tender feelings by asking about her infirmity. They were quite protective of her."

Caleb set his work aside, crouched by the stove, and added a fat log. "Then you were her only friend."

"Friend? No." She let her hurt show, hunching her shoulders and bowing her head. "You were correct. I was nothing but her servant." The blunt words sounded raw to her own ears, making her wonder if he'd caught her barely leashed ire. She tried to tamp it down, doing what she always did to unpleasant memories—whitewashing them until they hurt less. "At least by being close to Jacqueline I could share in her education. I can read, write, and cipher. Father Depardieu often shared his books with me. Which I suppose answers your question on why I speak so well. I was always around people who had manners and elocution. I simply copied them. I fear the only thing I didn't master was French. The Colberts insisted they were Americans and should speak English. They only slipped on occasion, usually when angry."

He stood behind her chair, rubbing the stiffness out of her shoulders.

Sara relaxed. The way his touch eased the sting in her muscles made her stop sewing. She closed her eyes and let him work his magic.

Caleb was having a hard time keeping his hands off his wife. At least she allowed his touch. Her neck and shoulders were knotted, but she softened with his touch. The rubbing turned to caressing, and when he brushed aside her braid and pressed a kiss to the side of her neck, she tilted her head, gave a little mewl, and let him play.

Her skin bore the scent of the rose petal soap, and he breathed in deeply. "You smell like heaven," he said, tracing the shape of her ear with the tip of his tongue.

She shivered in response.

Moving to stand in front of her, Caleb set Sara's sewing aside. Then he took her hands and pulled her to her feet. She came into his arms unbidden, and he smiled as he enfolded her in his embrace. "Where's Jacqueline now?"

Her whole body stiffened, making him curse in his mind. He should've left the topic alone. She'd said her piece. But no, he always had to push a little harder. He just couldn't understand why she wasn't still with the woman. They'd been raised together. Surely this Jacqueline Colbert would want to keep Sara close.

His mama always told him his unyielding curiosity would be the end of him.

"She died at eighteen," Sara replied. "Her mother blamed me."

"Why?"

"I should make some supper."

Although she might want to divert him from the topic, something important was hiding in this story—something beyond getting to know his bride. He wouldn't allow her to raise a shield. "Why did Mrs. Colbert blame you?"

"I caught a fever. Many of the servants did as well. When Jacqueline fell ill, she didn't recover. She died three weeks after taking to her sickbed. I was told I killed her."

"You did no such thing!"

Resting her forehead against his chest, she sighed. "I should've been more careful. The first cough. The first sneeze. I should have known to stay away. She was so...fragile. And then she was gone."

While Jacqueline and her parents had clearly seen Sara as nothing more than an indentured servant, Sara had loved Jacqueline. He could hear it in her every word. "Did you go back to your mama and papa?"

"I think I've lost my appetite. I'd like to bathe and then get some sleep."

Caleb squeezed her a little tighter against him. "Honesty, sweetheart. Remember? I–I need to know what happened to you."

"Why?" she whispered.

"'Cause I think you need to tell someone the truth about how you ended up here in White Pines."

She laid her cheek against his chest. "Mrs. Colbert wanted me tossed out, not even a scrap of clothing to go with me. After all I'd done...how I helped Jacqueline... She would've tossed me out like rubbish."

He stroked her hair, wanting to undo her braid so he could lace his fingers through the silky strands. "I'm so sorry."

As though she hadn't heard him, she pressed on. "Jean-Claude...um...Mr. Colbert kept me on as his...assistant."

Ah, but her tone betrayed her. She'd felt something for that man. "You loved him, didn't you?"

"Caleb, please... I don't wish to speak of that time or of him."

In all his life, Caleb had never felt jealousy over a woman. When Ty Bishop had courted Cassandra Shay, Caleb hadn't even been able to muster the emotion. That jealousy would seize him so swiftly and so strongly came as a surprise. But there it was, nevertheless, and although she hadn't confirmed his suspicions, he knew that this Jean-Claude had been her lover.

Was he the man who'd left the scars on her heart?

He hadn't realized she'd begun to cry until her muffled sob made him quit his questions. "I'm sorry, sweetheart. I shouldn't have hounded you."

When Sara pushed against him, he let her go. "I will explain. One day. I'm just...this has all happened so quickly. The trip from Denver and becoming your wife and—"

"Denver? How in the devil did Reverend Hayes find you in *Denver?* Told me he had plenty of ladies willing to come out here in his church in St. Louis."

Her eyes widened and she took several quick breaths. "W–who is Reverend Hayes?"

Caleb's stomach plummeted to his boots, and his heart slammed furiously against his ribcage. Something was wrong. Very wrong. "Reverend Hayes. The man who sent you out here to marry me."

Sara's hand flew to her mouth.

"Sara? Sweetheart? Didn't Reverend Hayes send you?"

She shook her head, eyes still as wide as a doe's.

They simply stood there, staring at each other as Caleb listened to his heartbeat thundering in his ears.

He'd made a mistake—a *huge* mistake. Sara hadn't come because of the money he'd sent with the good reverend.

Then where exactly *had* she come from?

"How did you know I wanted a wife?" His voice was hoarse with his fear.

"Oh, Caleb..." Tears pooled in her eyes and then spilled over her lashes. "I thought... I assumed... Sweet Lord, you weren't waiting for me. You were waiting for someone else." She wrapped her arms around her middle and moaned as though in pain. "We've made a big mistake."

Chapter Six

Near panic, Caleb needed her to explain. Quickly. "Answer me, Sara! Who told you I wanted a wife?"

Her anxiety was as clear as his own. Her hands trembled and her breathing sped. "No one. I came here because of my brother."

His stomach churned. "Your brother?"

"Ty. Ty Bishop."

Caleb picked up the block of wood he'd been carving and hurled it at the wall. "Bishop? *Bishop!* I should've known! That bastard!"

His history with Ty Bishop had been contentious since both men had sought Cassandra Shay's hand in marriage. Caleb had wanted a wife, and Cassie had been beautiful and smart and one of the few suitable single women he'd met in near to four years.

Was this some kind of revenge?

The way Sara stared at him, wide-eyed with a touch of fear, helped his senses slowly return.

Sending her to him hadn't been Ty's elaborate plan for revenge. What *revenge* was there in helping Caleb marry a woman like Sara? She was a *blessing.*

There were so many questions swirling through his mind he could barely grasp a single one. The most obvious came first. "Your name ain't Bishop."

"Ty uses our mother's maiden name."

"Why?"

"He hates our father. He would never claim himself to be a Fuller."

Caleb shook his head in dismay. He was caught in some trap, one designed by a man he disliked. Yet this trap had given him exactly what he wanted. So why was he even considering chewing off his own leg to get out of it?

Sara sank back into the chair, wringing her hands in her lap. "The stage. I should've... When you were there... Who is Reverend Hayes? What does he have to do with you marrying me?"

"Nothing. And everything."

Raking his fingers through his hair with an unsteady hand, he tried to figure out what to tell her. Sara was his wife—the marriage had been consummated. There was no going back, not unless he decided to pursue a divorce. That simply wasn't done. No one in White Pines would ever speak to him again. And Ty Bishop would have his head on a platter.

Hell, once Caleb let Ty know he'd wedded and bedded his sister without his permission, he'd be lucky if he didn't have an ugly feud on his hands. Sides would be taken, and Caleb feared most of the town would sympathize with Ty.

"Who's Reverend Hayes, Caleb?" She'd fisted her hands and pounded them against her thighs. "I need to know."

"I–I gave him money and a letter asking for a bride. He said he knew single women in St. Louis who'd love to come to Montana, that he'd find me a wife. I thought you were the woman he sent. I got a message a week ago sayin' she'd be here any day."

"That's why you were waiting on the stage. Oh, my God. I thought... I thought my brother had sent you." She popped to her feet and grabbed her coat. "I am a fool."

"What are you doing?"

"I'm going back to town."

"Don't be daft. It's dark. You got nowhere to go anyway."

Until she let out a shuddering breath, he hadn't realized she was close to tears. He went to her and gently took the coat from her hands to hang it back up. "Sara...you can't go."

She clutched for his hands. "This can be fixed, Caleb. I know it can. We've only been married a day. Surely the reverend who married us can just... I don't know... tear up the marriage certificate? We can all act as though this never happened."

Caleb could taste her fear, and he couldn't tell if that fear was because she'd married him and now wanted to escape—or was there something else dogging her heels, something she hadn't told him yet, something that would come to light when their marriage was revealed to her brother.

"There were other witnesses, Sara. And my brother was there. We can't pretend this marriage didn't happen. I don't want to pretend."

"I need to go," Sara insisted, her voice nearly hysterical. She pulled away to start pacing, turning in tight circles before pacing some more. The clip of her boot heels against the floor sounded much like the ticking of a grandfather clock. "We can make this right for you, Caleb. I'll do whatever I can to make this right for you."

"But you're my wife now. It's done. It can't be undone."

"A day. We've barely been married one day. There's nothing but a piece of paper binding us. The reverend will surely understand."

Caleb stepped in front of her, tugging her into his arms and holding her tight, relieved she didn't struggle. The rug had been pulled out from under him, and he wasn't sure exactly what his best choice was. All he knew was that as he'd sat there carving and watching his wife sew, a contentment the likes of which he'd never enjoyed before had settled over him. It had felt...*right*.

Sara Fuller might not have been the bride he'd expected to have, but she was the bride he'd gotten.

And he wasn't going to let her go.

He kissed the top of her head. "Listen to me, Sara. What's done is done."

"But—"

"Listen. Please."

She nodded and then rested her forehead against his chest.

"We've only been married a day, but we *are* married. Don't matter if it's a day or thirty years. The certificate might only be a piece of paper, but that ain't all binding us. We stated our vows before God. I ain't walking away from that commitment, and I ain't letting you walk away, neither."

Her chin rose until she was looking into his eyes. The fear hadn't vanished. "You don't know me, Caleb. I'm not what you wanted in a bride."

"You're exactly what I wanted. Young. Healthy. Strong. Ready to make a life with me on this farm." A rueful chuckle slipped out. "Didn't rightly want Ty Bishop as my brother-in-law, but I guess I gotta take the bad with the good."

Sara wasn't relaxing with his teasing. Instead, she slipped her hands between them and pushed against his chest. "You don't understand. You don't know me. I wasn't the woman you wanted...the one you planned for. We should end this."

When she tried to step back, he grabbed her by the waist. "Know what Ma always told me when I was growin' up?"

"Caleb, you have to let me go."

"Ma said everything happens for a reason. You're my wife now." He leaned in to brush a kiss over her frowning lips. "Let it be, sweetheart."

"But there was no reason for you to marry a woman like me."

Sara wanted to scream. She wanted to pound her fists against the walls and let loose of the anger and hurt coursing through her.

She should've known. Good things *never* happened to her. She was Sara Fuller—the woman who always seemed to court disaster. The moment Caleb told her he was there for her, she'd let herself believe that all the bad in her life had been left behind in Denver.

She'd been wrong.

Now she found herself in the life she'd always dreamed of with a handsome husband and hope for the future.

It was all a lie.

"We can fix this, Caleb." When she tried to pull away, he gripped her tighter.

"I don't wanna *fix this*, Sara. You're my wife."

"I'm not."

"You are."

He'd never understand if she didn't tell him the full truth, no matter how much it humiliated her. "Jean-Claude Colbert—"

"Was your lover," Caleb calmly finished her sentence.

Sara gasped. "How could you know that?"

The look he gave her seemed too much like pity. "I could hear it in your voice, in the way you talked about him." He let go of her waist long enough to stroke her cheek with the back of his knuckles. "You think you're the first young lady who gave her virtue to a man she thought she loved? Hell, Sara...the world's full of 'em. When you talked about him, I could tell."

She shook her head, but he grasped her chin.

"Know why Ma and Pa came all the way out here when they got rich?" he asked.

The question piqued her curiosity enough to allow a short distraction. "Why?"

"'Cause they thought cities destroyed people and they weren't gonna let that happen to them."

"You're speaking in riddles again..."

Caleb led her to the bedroom, sat on the bed, and dragged her down to sit beside him. Then he wrapped his arm around her shoulders. "I need to tell you 'bout Ma and Pa, and... Well, I hope you understand and don't judge 'em too harshly."

A little snort slipped out. After the life she'd led, there was no way she could judge another human being for any mistakes. "I won't. I promise."

"Pa left home in '49. He was only fifteen. His pa had left him, his ma, and his sister before Pa even got to know him. They were so damned poor, and once Pa got wind of the gold they'd found in California? He was hightailing it there faster than a jackrabbit."

Since some of her customers had been miners who'd come far too late to the party at Sutter Mill, she knew of the draw of gold. So many had gone in search of it. So few had found any.

Judging from the home Caleb's father had built, he'd been one of the few.

"Pa staked his claim and made his fortune. Then he met Ma." Caleb hesitated, pulling his arm away from her shoulders and grasping her hand. While he thought things over, he stroked her palm with his thumb.

Sara didn't pull away. This marriage would be ended soon enough, but she let his touch soothe her for now as he told the story of his parents. The fact he was sharing it told her he trusted her.

Honesty.

He'd asked for honesty.

But could she truly offer that to him?

"Ma was..." He let out an exaggerated sigh. "She was a whore, Sara."

A gasp slipped from her lips. "She told you this?"

Caleb gave her a brusque nod. "She weren't proud of it, but she and Pa told us 'cause they didn't want us to hear it from someone else. Said the past had a habit of sneakin' up behind a body and bitin' him in the a— um...backside."

Still aghast that a mother would reveal something so humiliating to her sons, all Sara could do was listen to the tale of another woman who'd walked the same treacherous path.

"She kept herself alive by selling herself. Pa met her, decided she was for him, and snatched her away from that life. He sold his claim— made another fortune selling it, mind you—and dragged her here. No one knew them in White Pines. No one judged 'em. He was one of the founding fathers, and he never once shared his past or Ma's with the others. He just helped build a town outta nowhere so he'd have a place to start with a clean slate."

He turned his head and nudged her chin up so she was staring in his eyes. "Everyone needs a chance at a new start, Sara. Even women who fall in love with the Jean-Claudes of the world."

At least this was something she could be honest about. "I did love him, you see. I knew he was married, and although he told me he'd leave his wife, I knew that would never happen. I let him...keep me in a place where he could come to see me at his leisure. I was no better than—"

"Don't." His hand squeezed her. "You don't have to say it."

She frowned before giving him a curt nod. "Then one day, he tired of me." Then he'd sent a man to drag her to The Palace after he sold her to Crazy Kate.

"That's why you came here."

Caleb was wrong. There was more. *Much more.*

Despite what he'd told her about his mother, Sara couldn't confess the rest of her sins. The notion that she'd be so much less worthy in his eyes turned her stomach. There would be forgiveness, of that she had no doubt. What she couldn't allow was any esteem he held for her to be lost.

Better to walk away and never return.

Ty would take her in. Surely he and Cassie would be generous, just as he'd promised in his letters. Once she made a home with them, she could watch Caleb from a distance.

His wife would come. One day. His *real* wife.

Why was that thought akin to ripping her heart right from her chest?

Because Sara had already accepted him as her husband. She'd let him be Lancelot to her Guinevere.

You foolish, foolish woman!

Hadn't she learned her lesson with Jean-Claude? Hadn't she been reminded of her lot in life daily when she'd been at The Palace?

Men couldn't be trusted. Ever. Their hearts were made of stone, and their affections nothing but fleeting affairs if truly felt at all.

Sara had been cursed with a woman's heart—one that felt and wept and bled. And somehow in the short time she'd spent with Caleb Young, she'd let him in, if only just a little.

"Sara?"

Reality was a slap to the face. "I must go. Tonight."

"You ain't heard a word I said!"

"You deserve—"

"I come from common stock," he insisted. "I don't deserve nothing but what I got. Pa and Ma made this home, but they weren't never more than what they were. A miner and a whore who got lucky. They never pretended to be educated. They never put on airs. They never looked down their noses at no one."

"Even a woman like—"

He squeezed her hand tightly. "I don't give a damn if you was that man's mistress. Don't you see? It don't matter to me. You're my wife. I want you to stay that way. I took vows with you, Sara Young. I mean to keep 'em and hold you to the vows you made."

His eyes held a desperation that touched her soul. She recalled his tales of loneliness and wanting, and in that moment, she made a decision to reach farther than she should have allowed herself.

But she did it anyway.

"Fine."

Caleb cocked his head. "Fine what?"

"Fine. I'll remain here and be your wife."

Chapter Seven

Sara shifted on the wagon's bench as each rut in the road jostled her. While the stagecoach might have been a bumpy ride, the wagon offered little comfort against the rugged road. Her backside felt fair abused, and the chill in the air made her cheeks sting. Thankfully, she'd found plenty of warm clothes among the stash in the trunk, so she wore a knit cap that protected her tender ears.

Caleb chuckled and patted her thigh. "Almost there. Ty built his house a ways away from the Twin Springs. He don't cotton much to company, but Cassie will be glad to know you made it safely from Denver."

Although Sara nodded, she wasn't so sure of the reception she'd get from her brother and his wife. Things hadn't turned out quite as she'd planned, although having Caleb as her husband was more than she'd ever allowed herself to imagine. She was supposed to come to Ty's home and perhaps find a job teaching or housekeeping, things she felt she'd be good at. Instead, she was here to introduce her brother to her new husband.

The house wasn't as big as Caleb's, but sitting on a plot of thick sod, a small stream of smoke curling from the chimney, it looked so homey. There'd been no snow the night before, but frost added sparkle to the roof and the grass, giving the home an ethereal glow. The surrounding trees were mostly pines, so no autumn colors framed the setting.

"He wanted you to come to White Pines, Sara." Caleb eased back on the reins, slowing the horses. "He'll be glad you're here."

"Perhaps," she replied. "Although I worry..."

"About how he'll react when he finds out we're married?"

She nodded as the wagon ground to a halt. Caleb climbed out and came around to lift her down. Before her feet had even touched the ground, the front door opened.

Ty took a step out, blocking a rather short woman who hovered behind him. Cassie, no doubt.

Ty was always an intense presence. So tall. His hair was a lighter brown than Sara's own, with blond highlights whereas hers held darker, ebony hues. It was a bit longer than the last time she'd seen him.

Caleb took Sara's hand, which made Ty's initial frown deepen. Then his blue eyes flew wide. "Sara? Is that you?"

She smiled as she nodded. "Yes, Ty. I'm finally here, just as you asked."

His gaze kept shifting between her and Caleb. "I can see that. What I don't know is what you're doin' with that varmint."

Caleb's hand clenched around hers. "She's my—"

"Not yet," Sara whispered, trying to keep her voice low enough Ty and Cassie couldn't hear. "Let me explain. Please."

"Sara?" Cassie pushed her way past Ty. Her light brown hair was loose around her shoulders, and her gait as she approached them could only be called a waddle, the child she carried putting quite a burden on her small body. "You're Ty's sister?"

"I am." Sara tossed one last gaze to Caleb and whispered, "Let me tell him in my own way. Please."

Her husband nodded and let her pull away. She met Cassie halfway and despite the size of the woman's belly, they embraced.

Sara rested her hand on Cassie's stomach. "I didn't know. When will the child come?"

"Soon," Cassie replied, putting her hand over Sara's. A smile reached her hazel eyes. "Only a week or so more."

Ty came up to his wife's side and draped an arm over her shoulder. "You shoulda told me you were coming."

"I simply didn't have the proper time to send word," Sara replied. "I–I need to speak to you. In private." She glanced back to Caleb, who'd stayed by the wagon but watched them with great interest. "About Caleb."

"Damn right we need to talk about him." Ty pulled his wife closer against his side. "You go inside, Cassie girl. Stay warm. Take Caleb with you."

Although she pursed her lips in irritation—probably at being dismissed—Cassie nodded. Then she gestured at Caleb. "Come inside, Caleb. I have some strong coffee for us."

As Cassie turned to go, Ty stopped her and touched his lips to hers. She went into the house with a smile.

Caleb stopped, his gaze capturing Sara's.

"It will be fine," she assured, lightly touching his fingers with hers.

He frowned at Ty.

Ty frowned back.

Then Caleb followed in Cassie's footsteps, shutting the door behind them.

Ty's scowl was now directed at Sara. "While I'm happy as a rabbit in fresh clover to see you, Sara...can't say I'm pleased to see you with Caleb Young."

Sara couldn't help but let out a laugh. "I dare say you shall have to become accustomed to him. You'll be seeing a lot of him whenever you see me."

His brown eyebrow arched.

"It's a long story, brother."

With a heavy sigh, he took her hand and dragged her to wooden bench right outside the door. Plopping down, he dragged her to sit next to him. "Start talkin'."

She started at a point in her odyssey she felt comfortable to relate. "I finally found the funds to come to you."

"Why didn't you send word?" he asked.

"As I said before, there simply wasn't time." While being totally open with Caleb wasn't something she would risk, she could be honest with Ty. "I–I fear I stole the money to make the journey."

"From Crazy Kate?"

Sara couldn't help but laugh at that notion. "Had I done that, I would not be drawing breath now. No, I robbed a cowboy."

"A customer?"

She replied with a curt nod.

"That don't explain why you're with Caleb Young."

"He was waiting for the stage when I arrived. He acted as though he was there for me. We stumbled through some misunderstandings—which now seems a bit serendipitous—and those drove our actions."

His brow furrowed. "Actions? What *actions?*"

"Please don't shout at me. Caleb believed he was there to meet his intended—that a wife was coming for him. From the greeting he gave me, I assumed you'd sent him for me, that you'd somehow arranged for me to have a husband and a home of my own."

"How in the hell could I send him for you? I didn't know you were coming."

"I see that now, Ty. I was so weary...and so frightened. I feared you and Cassie had decided I would be a burden and had convinced Caleb to take me in. He said all the right things..."

"Oh, I'll *bet* he did. Got you right into his bed, didn't he?"

She should've been offended, but she wasn't. A former whore had no right to be indignant when someone—even her own brother—assumed she'd conducted a little bit of business in return for a comfortable home. Hadn't she done exactly that? On a bathroom floor, no less.

She didn't deserve the luxury of outrage.

Ty wagged his finger at her. "Get this straight, Sara—you ain't gonna whore no more. I won't allow it. Caleb is gonna have to understand that you ain't sleeping with him again."

A rueful chuckle slipped out, and she allowed herself a moment of sarcasm in light of yet another misunderstanding. Seemed as though her life was filled with them lately. "I fear that I *will* be sleeping with him again."

Ty leapt to his feet. "I wanted you away from Denver so you didn't make you're your living on your back. You ain't a whore no more! Not for him! Not for any man!"

"You're correct. I'm not going to sell myself to Caleb or any other man ever again."

His angry growl made her drop the teasing. "Sara..."

"I'm his wife, Ty."

Her announcement promptly ended his growling, but the way he gaped at her made her feel as though she'd suddenly sprouted a second head. "His *what?*"

"His *wife*." Sara patted the bench beside her. "Sit back down, Ty. I'll tell you everything. Then it will be up to you and your wife to decide whether I'm still welcome in your home."

***

Caleb shook his head as he looked out the window yet again.

Sara had been talking to Ty for a very long time. The man wasn't even wearing a coat, yet he acted as though the cold didn't affect him. Caleb tried not to see that as a bad sign, but the minutes ticked by slowly as he worried Ty might be trying to convince Sara to end her marriage.

"You haven't touched your coffee, Caleb," Cassie called sweetly from where she leaned against the kitchen table.

With a sigh, he turned away from the window. "I'm sorry, Cassie. I'm just...worried."

She considered him over the rim of her mug as she sipped. "Ty just wants to understand the reasons Sara has finally decided to come to us. Perhaps you'd like to share the tale of how she came to be in your company? Ty will share the story with me once he hears it, but curiosity has me firmly in its grasp."

Although telling the whole tale to a woman who'd once been the focus of his romantic attention would be embarrassing, Caleb sat down and sipped from the coffee she'd poured for him before beginning. "Sara came three days ago. Arrived on the afternoon stage, and I was there to meet it."

"Meet it? Why on earth would you have been waiting for Ty's sister to arrive? We didn't even know she was coming."

He couldn't help but smile. Seeing Cassie confused made him feel less moronic. "I was waiting for someone else, but I didn't know it."

"Stop talking in circles, Caleb. I want to hear everything."

"Do you know what a mail-order bride is?"

She nodded, holding the cup in her hands as if trying to absorb some of the coffee's warmth.

"Remember when Reverend Hayes came visiting?"

"I do. The man was quite charismatic. How does one topic relate to the other?"

"He got wind of me wantin' a bride, you see...and well, we...talked about some of the women back in his home in St. Louis. He suggested that he could...um...persuade one to come to White Pines and be my wife."

Cassie's eyes widened. "Caleb, you didn't!"

He cheeks heated as he nodded.

"I had no idea you were so...so..."

"Desperate?"

"You're only twenty-what? Four?"

"Twenty-five last birthday. Old enough to know my own mind." He rolled his eyes. "You don't know my life, *Mrs. Bishop*. You got everything you wanted and can share it with someone. I got nobody."

"Gideon—"

A snort slipped out. "Gideon's my brother, Cassie. He and Drew are family. What I want is a companion—someone to be there when I wake up and sleepin' by my side each night. Someone who'll help me through my cares and woes and share the good in life." Caleb gave her a weary sigh. "I want what you got, and I thought the good reverend could help me get it. If that makes me a fool, so be it."

Cassie set her cup down. "You're no fool. You're simply lonely. I find no fault in your actions, I was simply surprised."

"Surprised? Hell, don't you remember I was gonna try to strong-arm you into marrying me even though you didn't love me?"

"I suppose you did do that. But I hadn't considered your proposal was born of loneliness." She pulled out one of the kitchen chairs and nodded toward another. "Sit. Please."

He obliged her, sitting down as he set aside his cup. "The reverend sent me word a few days back that a woman had agreed to come to me. He said she wanted to meet me first—to see if we got along. If we did, she'd agree to be my wife." Uncomfortable with the way he'd rushed Sara through the wedding, he winced. "Didn't honor that promise and give Sara a moment to think it over. Rushed her right to the altar 'cause I didn't want to lose her."

Her lips thinned into a grim line. "Did you send money with the reverend, Caleb?"

"I did."

"You weren't afraid he would pocket it and forget all about his promise?"

"Of course I was." He shrugged. "But he's a man of God. If you can't trust a man of God, then there ain't nobody you can trust."

"I had no idea things were that bad." Cassie's tone held a little too much pity for Caleb's taste.

"Ain't wantin' you to feel sorry for me," he insisted.

"I don't," she retorted. "I was merely thinking about the other men who feel as you do. I hadn't stopped to consider how many of our friends in town might be every bit as lonely. Perhaps we should work as a community to encourage more women to come here."

"You know, I've heard of that happening. Churches sending pictures of the men wantin' wives and letting 'em pick. Then the men pay for passage to get 'em there."

"Well then...we shall have to bring the subject up at the next town meeting."

Before Caleb could reply to that rather bold suggestion, the door opened. Sara stepped inside, followed closely by Ty. A frown on his face, the man didn't appear any happier than he'd been before the conversation with his sister.

Caleb went to Sara and helped her take off her coat.

"Let me get you some hot coffee to warm you." Cassie awkwardly tried to stand.

Ty was quickly at her side, grabbing her elbow and helping the expectant mother to her feet.

She smiled and murmured her thanks.

Caleb lowered his head to his wife and whispered, "Everything okay?"

"We can discuss it on our way home," Sara replied in the same quiet tenor.

Her words worried him. "Ain't nothing to discuss. We're married now, and we're staying that way."

After she pulled off her gloves, she took his hand. "Yes, Caleb. We're staying married."

Cassie held up a cup. "Please come take this, Sara. I fear much of the liquid will spill over the sides should I try to bring it to you."

Relieved that Caleb accepted her pledge, Sara went to her sister-in-law. "Thank you, Cassie." The warm mug felt wonderful against her chilled hands.

A silence settled over the four of them, making her nerves begin to fray. What she needed desperately was acceptance, and now that Ty knew about her marriage, she worried that he regretted tendering his invitation to have her come to Montana.

Inclining his head at Caleb, Ty stared down at his wife. "Sara married him."

"So I was told." Cassie eased herself back into the chair with Ty's help. "I'm very happy for them, Ty."

"Happy?" He snorted. "Never expected my sister to marry a Young."

"Yes, *happy*," she replied in a scolding tone. "Sara needs Caleb every bit as much as Caleb needs her. I think it will be a sound union."

"Why?"

"Because two good people have found their ways to each other," she declared. "And I, for one, believe that is a bit of a miracle." Cassie tossed Sara a genuine smile. "Besides, Sara Young has a nice ring to it, don't you think?"

Ty might have expressed a few reservations about Sara's marriage, but he'd agreed to accept Caleb as her husband. And Cassie's words let Sara know she was welcome.

With a smile, she let her fears go.

She'd found the acceptance she'd needed.

Chapter Eight

"Sara, sweetheart? Sara? Wake up. I need you..." Caleb's voice called to her as though from a distance, the rest of his words lost to the haze of her lingering slumber.

She barely opened her eyes, reaching up to cup his beard-roughened face in her palm.

This wasn't the first time she'd dreamt about him since they'd married. The passing week had been full of him—both day and night.

While the sun was up, she followed him like a faithful puppy as he taught her the chores necessary to run their farm. His hands had covered hers as she squeezed the cow's teats to make milk shoot into the bucket—or into the mouths of the barn cats, much to Sara's delight. He'd helped her gather eggs each morning and feed the animals a couple of times a day, and they'd talk about everything and nothing.

He'd followed through with his promise to help her ride, sitting behind her on Mate as he taught her the proper way to hold the reins. After only a couple of lessons, she conquered the skill and her fear.

Because of him.

At night, Caleb held her in his arms as she drifted off to restful sleep. He never pushed her for intimacies, although he kissed her often. Their late night kisses were the sweetest, and although she'd made it plain she'd give him his husbandly rights, he never took her up on the offer. He always said he knew she'd *allow* more, but he wanted her to *want* more. What came as a surprise was that with each kiss they shared, desire took root inside her. Her body was slowly awakening, feeling things she'd never felt before. Those new sensations both excited and frightened her.

She was beginning to believe she truly *did* want more.

If only she could toss aside the shackles of fear that still lingered, the memories of the men who'd taken her before that hovered like spirits in her head. They were sluggishly fading into nothing but mists of the past, but until they were gone, she couldn't ask her husband for more than kisses.

Even when dreams claimed her, Caleb was still there. Her sweet knight. Kissing her. Holding her. Making her feel safe.

He would help banish the spirits.

One day...

She caressed his cheek. "I need you too, Caleb."

"Wake up," he coaxed, putting his hand over hers and rubbing his cheek against her palm. "I need you to see this. I've been waitin' the longest time..."

"Anything," she said. "I'll do anything for you." Threading her fingers through his thick, dark hair, she stopped him from pulling back. Then she kissed him—the first time she'd initiated a kiss.

Soon, the brush of lips made her restless, sending chills racing over her skin that had nothing to do with the cool air. The way her body responded to him still surprised her, but now that response had her wide awake and made heat pool between her thighs.

With a low moan, Caleb crawled onto the bed and covered her body with his as he teased his tongue past her lips.

Sara lost herself in the feel of his warm, soft lips and the weight of his body. Never had she believed she'd crave a man on top of her. Yet even though there were quilts between them, he felt right as he lay on her. He shielded some of his weight by supporting himself on his elbows, a courtesy that she simply wasn't accustomed to. His consideration allowed her arms to slip around his neck so she could arch into him.

He tore his lips away to kiss and lick the sensitive spot behind her ear. "God, Sara... I want you so damn bad."

"Then have me."

With a low groan, he eased back. "When you're ready."

"I'm ready, Caleb."

He shook his head. "Not yet. Soon. C'mon, sweetheart. Get up. I wanna show you something."

The sleep now cleared from her mind, she frowned. He was bundled up as if the winter cold had invaded their home. "Why are you wearing your coat?"

"I told you. I wanna show you something."

"What time is it?" She didn't feel at all rested. Only the moonbeams spilling through the window gave off any light. Why was he dressed so in the middle of the night?

All he did was shrug.

"Is it one of the animals?" She tossed aside the quilt and sucked in her breath as the cold air washed over her. "Is a cow ill?"

"No." Caleb picked up her coat from where he'd draped it over the end of the bed. "It's something really special."

In no time, he had her bundled up. Then he took her by the hand and dragged her out the front door.

"Where are we going?" Sara asked as she stumbled beside him in his march across the snowy field to the north of their house.

"Just a little farther. Gotta get past the trees to see it proper."

"See what?"

"My surprise. No more questions, wife. Trust me and be patient."

"I dare say that is not one of my virtues."

His laughter floated in little white tufts through the cold night air.

Mouth agape in surprise, Sara saw it right before Caleb said, "Look!"

Never would she have imagined a sky could be so beautiful. Colors painted an arc rising from the mountains and looking much like flames shooting from the tall pines. Pink. Purple. Green. All dancing in a mixture of bright swirls and ribbons of light.

"It's...*amazing*," she whispered in reverence.

"Ain't it? Saw it for the first time when I weren't more than a sprout. Come out here in the middle of night from time to time just to see if it's back. Tonight is one of the prettiest nights I've ever seen."

Pretty didn't come close to describing the view. "I've never seen anything so incredible." She stepped in front of him and smiled. "I'm humbled you chose to share it with me."

His smile made her stomach flip-flop. "You're welcome."

Slowly, he lowered his head, and knowing he was going to kiss her, Sara surrendered and closed her eyes. The kiss against her forehead made her open them in shock.

Why hadn't he kissed her?

He'd never seemed so reticent before. There were kisses all day long, kisses she now realized she'd come not only to expect and enjoy but to *need*. To her, each kiss revealed a closeness that was growing between them and represented the tethers he'd put on himself not to use her again. Because of those kisses, she'd started to trust Caleb in a way she'd never trusted another man.

When he'd touched his lips to her forehead instead of her mouth, she'd been sorely disappointed.

Caleb had to bit his lip not to smile at the disgruntled frown on his wife's face. Not that he'd be laughing at her... No, the smile would be because of his happiness.

Sara had wanted him to kiss her.

That pleased him more than she would ever know.

"Your skin is like ice," he said. "We should both get back to bed before we freeze to death."

He gave her no choice, sweeping her into his arms and carrying her back to their house. Although he felt a little guilty for having awakened her from such a sound sleep, he'd hoped she would see the beauty of the night lights that came to the mountains from time to time. He was no artist, but even he enjoyed the mix of colors and hoped Sara did as well.

Sharing his life had been more than he'd hoped for. His new wife was an eager student, learning quickly all the things that kept the small farm alive. When he'd decided to use any means he could to acquire a bride, he'd been thinking as much with his cock as his brain.

Now that she was here, his cock wasn't nearly as important. Not that it didn't notice her. Hell, he spent more time hard than he did soft. His desire for her sometimes stole his breath away. But he'd begun to realize just how important her company was. Her conversation. Her laughter. Her companionship.

She'd never denied him her body—he denied himself. He woke up all asweat some nights, rolling over to pull her closer as he kissed her. All that remained between them was her nightgown and his nightshirt. Tempting though it was to cast those frustrating garments aside and bury himself deep inside her, Caleb never gave in to those urges.

He wanted her to come to him.

Ah, but tonight she had!

Tonight, he'd caught her with her guard down in those moments where slumber dimmed her deeper thoughts. She'd kissed him. And in that moment, he'd nearly lost his control. Had he not been dressed in so many layers, he might've seduced her, hoping again to know the joy he'd found on that bathroom floor.

Yet that joy had been diminished because she hadn't shared in it.

Back in the house, he let Sara open the door, then he carried her through. He didn't set her on her feet until he reached their bed. Crouching, he doffed his gloves, boots, and coat and then helped her remove her boots. Her legs were bare since he'd urged her to follow him too quickly to don stockings.

Her soft skin, pale in the moonlight, was hypnotic, and Caleb slid his fingertips up the flesh of her calves.

She shivered. From the cold or his touch, he wasn't sure—didn't really even give it a care for his plan had already taken form in his thoughts.

Rising, he unbuttoned her coat, brushing it from her shoulders to let it drop to the floor next to his.

Sara stood statue-still until his hands covered her breasts. Then she began to tremble as her nipples hardened beneath his touch.

Caleb didn't allow himself to linger there, wanting to overwhelm her in a way he knew she'd never experienced. He didn't consider himself much of a lover, but his wife had only known possession of that Frenchman who'd probably treated her in the manner a master treated a slave. She'd never been with someone who gave her pleasure simply for the desire of watching her enjoyment.

He vowed she would learn that tonight.

Allowing himself one luxury, he tore off his shirt and whipped her nightgown over her head, wanting to be skin to skin with her. He dare not remove his trousers, aware that there would be nothing to stop him from taking her if that barrier didn't remain.

Tugging her into his arms, Caleb kissed her—a kiss that he filled with the hunger that gnawed at him. His tongue stroked hers, claiming the sweetness of her mouth. The way her tongue returned the caress emboldened him, letting him know that he was right.

She was ready for *more*.

But not for *all*.

Tearing his mouth away, he lowered his head to pull the tight bud of a nipple into his mouth, suckling as she tangled her fingers in his hair and let out a small cry. He shifted to her other breast, loving how she tugged at his locks and arched into him.

She didn't know yet what he intended for her, and he smiled against the soft skin between her breasts. With no warning, he lifted her into his arms and laid her against the linens so her legs dangled over the side of the bed. Spreading her thighs, he kissed his way down her flat stomach.

"Caleb...?"

He rose over her again, giving her one hard kiss. "Let me play, wife. I promise to please you."

"It is I who should be pleasing you."

"Then you're in luck." Another quick kiss. "Because this pleases me."

Caleb traced her collarbone with his tongue as he slipped a hand to the juncture of her thighs. She clenched her legs together, but he simply eased them apart with his knee and explored her with his fingers.

Sara gasped at the feel of his hands teasing and probing. His journey of kisses down her body was detoured when he drew her nipple between his teeth and tugged. She hissed in a breath and let the heat of his touch burn straight through her.

It had never been like this before. No man had ever taken the time to coax her body to respond. Even Jean-Claude had seemed more concerned with his own agenda than whether she was a participant in the act.

She'd been nothing to the men who came before her husband. Nothing but a lump of flesh.

Caleb made her feel more—so much more. Cherished. Desired. Needed.

His tongue circled her navel before his fingers separated her folds and his mouth was suddenly...*there*.

"No. You musn't..." She squirmed, trying to stop him.

He held tight to her hips and brushed a kiss against her inner thigh. "I must. Let me have my way. I promise this is for you."

The words made no sense. Men had often asked her to use her mouth on their bodies, even offering to pay more. But she'd always refused. It was the same with kisses. They were too intimate for her to share with a man she'd not see again until the next payday.

"For you...this is for *you*," she insisted. It was the only explanation that she could find for what he was suggesting.

"I ain't gonna lie. I'll like it right fine. But trust me, Sara, I do this for *you*." He dipped his head back between her thighs and loved her with his mouth.

Only a few strokes of his tongue and she surrendered. Her body betrayed her, growing taut with desire like she'd never experienced. Heat surged through her, flowing like fire through her veins. She drew her knees up, opening herself to him and receiving more pleasure than she'd dreamed of in return.

Caleb's fingers joined the assault on her senses, finding a spot so tender and full of heat that her heels dug into the mattress as she raised her hips in rhythm with the moving of his tongue over the sensitive flesh.

Her muscles tightened, a knot settling in her lower belly. "Caleb...please..."

Her pleas seemed to spur him on. A finger slipped deep inside her as he tugged at the nub of flesh with his teeth.

Sara shattered, crying out in wonder and surprise as waves of pleasure washed over her. She pulled his hair and called his name until the spasms began to subside.

And then he was gone, hurrying away before she could stop panting like a well-run horse.

When her senses returned, she snatched up the quilt, wrapped it around herself and went to find out where her husband had gone.

A groan came from the bathroom, so she headed there, skidding to a stop when she saw him.

Caleb stood with an arm braced against the wall, a washing cloth clenched in his fingers. His head was bowed, his eyes closed. His pants were bunched around his ankles, and his hand moved over his erect cock, pumping up and down the length in a fast, steady cadence.

She was hypnotized by him. The strength of his body in the moonlight rendered her mute. Roped muscle was covered with skin that gleamed a ghostly white. Her sated body leapt back to life, and for the first time in far too long, she looked on a man's body with a flicker of desire rather than fear.

Another groan slipped from his lips as his hand sped its rhythm. Suddenly, he threw his head back, held the washing cloth over the end of his cock, and grunted her name.

She damned the floorboards that squeaked as she tried to ease away before he saw her.

Caleb's eyes flew wide and he scrambled to pull up his pants. "Sara... I'm so sorry—"

"Stop," Sara replied, holding up her hand. "I was...intruding. I'm the one who should apologize." She inclined her head in dismissal and backed away to return to the bedroom.

She'd donned her nightgown and was sandwiched between the covers when her husband returned to her.

With no words, he tugged on his nightshirt, shed his pants, and joined her. As usual, he pulled her against him, fitting his body around hers in a way that always made her feel safe.

Sleep refused to come. Her mind was too full of feelings and images that refused to abate. Finally, she had to ask, "Why?"

"Hmm?"

"Why did you...do *that?*"

He nuzzled his nose against her braid and then chuckled. "Which *that?* The that I did to you, or the one I did to myself?"

Since her curiosity knew no bounds, and she'd already been as embarrassed as she ever thought possible, she gave in and said, "Both, I suppose."

"I did that to you because I wanted to make you happy. And I did, didn't I, Sara?"

"Yes," she confessed. "I never knew it could be that...splendid." There seemed to be no words to explain how he'd made her body sing. If that was the pleasure men received whenever they spilled their seed, it was no wonder Crazy Kate made so much money.

"As for what you found me doing... I had to."

"Why?"

"'Cause I couldn't be inside you. Not yet."

Sara tried to look at him over her shoulder. "But why? I've not refused you."

"Like I told you, sweetheart... I want you to want me first."

The biggest revelation of a night full of them was that in the moment before her release, she *had* wanted him. Her body had craved the feel of him filling her completely.

Or had she been too confused and overwhelmed to know exactly what she wanted?

She let this statement stand without more comment.

Caleb kissed her cheek, and she settled her head back against her pillow. "You were so sweet, Sara. All female and sugar and I ain't got a lot of control. I had to give in to the urge. Forgive me."

"Forgive you?"

"If what you saw was too shocking, I'm sorry."

While she wanted to tell him she was a whore—that nothing

shocked her—she refrained. Every day with Caleb made her feel less like the disgrace she'd been and more like a human being with value—at least to him.

Maybe someday she'd value herself as well.

Chapter Nine

Gideon climbed out of the wagon and leveled a hard stare at Sara.

She stood her ground and held tight to her husband's hand as she straightened her spine. For near to two weeks, she'd enjoyed the peace of the farm. Working at her husband's side had made her feel as though she'd finally found somewhere she belonged, and she had no intention of giving it up. Even for a disapproving brother-in-law.

But that one big obstacle remained—she wanted Gideon's approval. Until he accepted Sara as Caleb's wife, she'd never truly find happiness. Something she wanted with all her heart.

Another man made his way out of the wagon. He was a handsome devil. Blond. Blue-eyed. His smile was every bit as charming as that of an enticing salesman. She hoped that smile wasn't every bit as false.

While Gideon went to Caleb to cuff him on the shoulder, the blond moved directly in front of Sara. "I am Andrew Pearson. Drew to family members." He gripped her upper arms, dragged her close, and then kissed both of her cheeks. "Welcome to the family, Mrs. Young."

Caleb put himself between them so quickly, she didn't even see him coming. His arm swiped down, breaking the gentle hold Drew had on her. "Enough of that," Caleb snapped.

"Why, I have no idea what you're talking about," the man insisted with a lopsided smile that belied his words.

Why was he attempting to incite Caleb's anger?

"What are you tryin' to prove, Drew?" Caleb asked as though he'd read her mind.

"I wasn't trying to prove anything," Drew insisted. "I was merely attempting to make Sara feel welcome." He shot a rather stern frown at Gideon. "I was led to believe Gideon had failed to let her know how pleased he was that she is now your wife. Isn't that right, Gideon?"

A laugh slipped out before she could stop it, not only at Drew's teasing but because Gideon's face had reddened so quickly at the pleasant scolding.

Drew tossed her a smile. "So I was correct? You weren't made welcome?"

"I dare say I wasn't," she replied, keeping a wary eye on Gideon. While Drew seemed like a very open man who enjoyed witty banter, she feared Gideon was still angry that Caleb had married her the day she arrived.

Their marriage had enough obstacles. She hoped the hostility Gideon had shown could be set aside and they could start over. Only then would there be peace in the family.

"But I understand his concern," Sara added. "Were I to find my brother wed so hurriedly, I'd caution him that those who marry in haste often repent in leisure."

Gideon doffed his hat and ran his hand over his face. "I was just surprised. Okay? I didn't expect him to really get a mail order bride. Thought that reverend was laughing all the way back to St. Louis with Caleb's money burning a hole in his pocket. Thought Caleb had been fleeced like a sheep in summer."

Sara winced, looking to her husband to see if he was going to correct the misassumption. She hated lying to Gideon and Drew. They'd surely discover the truth of that situation soon. The whole town would figure out she wasn't the bride Caleb had expected on that stage. Wouldn't the news be better learned from Caleb than through distorting gossip?

Caleb took her hand in his and squeezed. "I should tell him," he whispered.

"I agree," she replied.

"Tell me?" Gideon cocked his head. "Tell me what?"

"Sara didn't come from the reverend."

"Beg your pardon?" Drew said, furrowing his brow.

Gideon was less genteel. "What the hell does that mean?"

"The reverend didn't send her," Caleb replied. "Ty Bishop did."

The surprised expression on Gideon's face was entertaining. Sara watched him closely to memorize his features. Whenever she needed a smile, she could pluck that shocked image from her memory for it would surely amuse her as much in the future as it did at that moment.

Gideon shook his head. "B–but... I thought... I mean... Don't you hate Ty Bishop?"

"Hate is a rather harsh word." Drew's gaze had settled on Sara, as though he were searching for the truth. "Ty Bishop, eh? You know I do believe I see the family resemblance. So tell us, sweet Sara... How did you come to find yourself at the altar with our Caleb?"

She let her gaze settle on Caleb, hoping he'd again take the lead. Instead, he quirked a dark eyebrow.

With an inward sigh of resignation, she told what she could. "Ty and I were separated at a very early age, as most of our siblings were. Our parents were quite poor, you see. Only a few years ago, our oldest sister went to great effort to hunt us down and allow us to get to know each other again. I was the hardest to find, but Ty eventually tracked me to Denver." *Where he found me working at The Palace and decided to save me from the life of a whore...*

Drew grinned. "And so he tendered an invitation for you to come to our fair town? Correct?"

Sara nodded, not bothering to share Ty's concern for her health and safety. He'd all but dragged her right out of the brothel, the only thing preventing that being the barrel of Crazy Kate's shotgun aimed at his heart. But his desire to save her had sparked a yearning inside her to save herself. "I accepted his invitation."

"Obviously," Gideon drawled, drawing a sharp glare from Drew.

Caleb took over the telling. "Got a telegram a few days before she got here that the reverend had found me a bride, so I was waitin' on the stage that day. Sara stepped off, and... well..." He shrugged and tensely rubbed the back of his neck.

She filled in the rest. "We had a series of rather amusing misunderstandings that found me thinking Ty had sent Caleb to me and Caleb believing I'd come to be his bride. So much went unsaid, causing us to reach the wrong conclusions."

"And yet," Drew said, "it led you to the right place for I dare say Caleb has never appeared quite so happy or content." He reached for Sara's hand, lifted it, and kissed the back of her knuckles, making her cheeks warm. "Kismet has brought you two together, sweet Sara. It was fate. There is no other explanation."

Although she thought the statement a bit too romantic, she nodded. The truth was a bit more sordid, and she thought about her becoming Caleb's wife as nothing more than a comedy of errors. If Drew wanted to call it "kismet," she wouldn't argue with him.

Even if she knew better.

"Thank you," she murmured. Caleb's eyes had grown stormy, and she didn't think it was a good idea to incite his jealousy.

Jealousy? That thought hit her hard. Was her husband shooting daggers at Drew with his gaze because he didn't like seeing another man touch her?

A passing thought drifted through her mind. If another woman had the temerity to touch Caleb, she'd be tempted to slap the hussy.

Marriage was turning out to be more complicated than Sara had ever anticipated. When she'd stood before the preacher, holding Caleb's hands as she stated her vows, she'd imagined cooking, cleaning, and living with one man. Of course she'd be giving him free use of her body because she was, after all, his lawful wife. But even that wouldn't be enough to steal away her contentment.

Instead, her husband had changed the rules. He worked every bit as hard on the farm and keeping the home as she did, claiming he loved being at her side regardless of the task. Although she'd made it plain he could indulge his masculine urges, he hadn't touched her for his own pleasure. Whenever he reached for her, he had focused on giving her pleasure, something she was quickly learning to crave.

His selflessness had won her loyalty.

Caleb snatched her hand away from Drew, who still smiled as though he thoroughly enjoyed the possessive reaction. "We need to get inside and outta this cold." He dragged her to the house.

"Wait," Gideon said. "Please. I'd like a minute alone with Sara."

Caleb pulled her closer, suspicious of his brother's motives. Gideon had made it clear from the moment he'd met Sara that he didn't approve of her. What could he possibly wish to say to her that he couldn't say in front of him or Drew?

Out of habit, he looked to Drew. Although the relationship between Gideon and Drew was unconventional, Caleb had learned to be happy that they'd found each other. The townsfolk never talked openly about the men, choosing instead to accept them as a pair of confirmed bachelors who decided to share a home to keep away the loneliness.

Gideon had always been such a serious fellow, probably because so much responsibility had been thrust upon him when their parents had died. The older brother became the man of the family and did a good job of raising Caleb, and for that he was eternally grateful. But there was also concern that Gideon would never know the pleasant parts of life or the love of a good woman.

In Gideon's case, what had saved him was the love of a good man.

Drew—Andrew Pearson—had stumbled into Gideon's life when he'd arrived in Twin Springs with Cassandra Shay, now Cassandra Bishop. The attraction between the men had been plain from the moment they met, and Caleb had welcomed Drew as soon as he saw the way Gideon opened up his tender emotions to the man. Thanks to Drew, Gideon had cast aside some of the solemnness that had haunted him. He smiled. He laughed. He enjoyed life.

Drew shifted his gaze from Caleb to Gideon and then back to Caleb. Then he gave him a curt nod.

"Well, then..." Caleb brushed a kiss over Sara's cheek. "I reckon Gideon can have his say." He leveled a hard stare at his brother. "Mind your manners, and remember...she's my wife by the laws of God and man. There ain't nothing you can do to change that."

"I don't want to change that," Gideon said, shifting nervously on his feet.

"Truly?" Caleb couldn't help but be surprised. The last time he'd seen his brother, Gideon had been ranting and raving about the speed in which Caleb took Sara as his wife.

Why the change of heart?

Gideon nodded.

Drew nudged Caleb with his shoulder. "Come with me, Caleb. We shall let them have a moment to hash out their differences and clear the air."

With a worried glance back to Sara, Caleb let Drew lead him into the house.

***

Sara flinched when the door closed. She didn't want to be alone with Gideon. Not that she feared him, but her marriage was never going to be strong if her brother-in-law didn't accept her in Caleb's life.

The way Gideon stared at her now made her relax. There was something different about his gaze, something that was slowly helping her worry subside.

He leaned back against the small picket fence for the pen holding the two pigs Caleb was raising. Both of the pink piglets had been runts that he'd had to hand feed to keep alive. Since then, she'd taken over their care, naming them Tweedle Dee and Tweedle Dum after a wonderful poem she'd learned as a child. Only after she'd taken them to her heart as pets did Caleb inform her they were to be slaughtered for food. Her tears had swayed him, and now the pigs would be breeding stock rather than the salted pork they'd eat next winter.

Farm life wasn't going to be easy on her heart.

"Come and talk to me, Sara," Gideon said, beckoning with his gloved hand. "It's cold, so I ain't gonna be long. I just need to speak my mind."

She went to the fence, turned, and leaned back against the rails. Afraid to reveal her concern, she said nothing. He would have to speak first so she could gauge whether this conversation was going to be confrontational. Her nature was to assume the worst, so she made sure her feet were firmly on the ground in case she needed to escape.

"I ain't gonna bite you," he grumbled.

"What did you wish to say to me?" she asked.

He heaved a sigh and then pushed off the fence to come around and face her. "I wanted to tell you I was sorry."

"Sorry?"

"Yeah... It weren't right to yell at you, 'specially on your wedding day. I was just...so...so..."

"Surprised?"

His nod was accompanied by a small grin. "Never once thought Caleb would get himself a wife. Figured he'd have a better chance of panning for gold and making a fortune."

The need to defend Caleb swelled inside her, making her fear she'd lost the battle to keep him from reaching her heart. "He's a good man, a handsome man. Any woman would be lucky to be his wife."

"I like that," Gideon said with a firm nod.

"Pardon?"

"I like that you ain't gonna let nobody talk ill of him."

The conversation wasn't going anywhere close to the road she'd expected it to travel. "I only speak the truth."

"There's only one thing that bothers me," he said, his eyes searching hers.

"Oh?"

"You're holding some secrets inside you, Sara. I can see it all over your face."

She simply shrugged. Of course she had secrets. What adult didn't? Life was too difficult a journey to not have left behind a skeleton or two in the closets along the way.

"But I'm willin' to give you the benefit of the doubt," he added.

Sara knit her brows, not entirely sure if this was a reprieve or a warning. "I don't understand."

"I know all 'bout holding in secrets, Sara."

Such a simple statement that bore a wealth of feeling. She decided to offer him something she so desperately wanted from him. "If you are referring to what you share with Mr. Pearson, then I hope you realize I hold no ill will in that regard."

"Caleb told you 'bout Drew and me?" His tone bordered on panic.

She tried to ease his mind. "Yes, but please know that your secret is safe with me. I would never discuss family matters with outsiders. I will do my utmost to protect you from malicious gossip."

"That's mighty kind of you, 'specially after the way I acted."

"You are forgiven, Gideon."

"If you can swear to me that whatever secret you're keepin' ain't gonna come sniffing 'round Caleb, I ain't gonna hold it against you no more."

Crazy Kate had accepted Sara's leaving. The only true danger was Drake, the cowboy she'd robbed. No matter how angry he'd been when he awoke to discover she'd stolen the payroll, there was no way he could track her to White Pines. If all Gideon wanted was assurance that her past would remain in her past, she felt safe giving him that promise.

"I swear."

He took her hands in his. "Welcome to the family, Sara Young."

Chapter Ten

"That was a fine supper, Sara." Caleb patted his rather full belly. "You sure took to cookin' like a tadpole to water."

Sara smiled back at him, making him smile in return.

She'd settled in nicely in his opinion. Farm life agreed with her, and despite the winter cold, she was thriving in Montana. Having her near not only eased the burden of caring for the animals, she was great company and filled what had been endless, empty hours talking about the stories she'd read. He'd already decided to buy her a book for Christmas. The problem was going to be finding a title she hadn't already devoured.

His loneliness was a thing of the past. Sara was now the bright light in his life.

There was only one obstacle remaining to Caleb's peace of mind. He still wanted Sara to not just *accept* him in her bed but *want* him there. He'd noticed subtle signs that he was drawing closer to his goal. From the softening in the way she spoke of their future and her plans for their home to the way she'd grown more affectionate, offering kisses and hugs for no real reason, gave him hope.

His wooing was going well, and he'd uncovered a passion inside her that he craved to share. But her desire couldn't be forced. He'd have to keep up his tender assault on her senses, hoping that soon she'd reach for him for more than a peck on the lips or a quick embrace. He longed for her to ask him to make love to her. When that joyous event occurred, he'd be the most contented man in the territory.

"Can I offer you boys a shot of whiskey?" Caleb asked, pulling the curtain aside to check the weather. Being polite was a habit, but what he really wanted was for Gideon and Drew to go back home so he could set himself back to winning over his wife. "It might brace you for the cold ride home."

Gideon shook his head. "We need to be leaving."

Drew went to Sara, took her hand, and kissed her knuckles. "Thank you for the wonderful supper and the pleasant conversation, Sara. I enjoyed the evening, as did Gideon. We are blessed to have you in our family."

Despite knowing Drew's preferences and how much he loved Gideon, Caleb wanted to punch him in the nose.

Jealousy was new to him, and it appeared the emotion was controlling him more than he was controlling it. He was able to harness his anger when he noticed how quickly Sara withdrew her hand and came to stand at Caleb's side.

"Thank you, Drew," she replied. "I enjoyed the evening as well."

Caleb tried not to read too much into the situation when she nudged his hand as if she wanted him to hold hers. He obliged her, giving her fingers a gentle squeeze.

"Bundle up," he said. "Snow's coming down mighty hard now. Ain't gonna be a fun ride home."

Gideon had already put on his heavy coat and was handing Drew's to him. "Think we're in for a storm?"

Caleb shrugged. "Skies are hard to read, but I ain't thinkin' blizzard. I'd say we're in for more than a few inches."

"How can you foretell the weather?" Sara asked, her beautiful blue eyes wide with curiosity.

He shrugged again while Gideon said, "Caleb's got a knack for readin' the winds and the clouds. Seems to always know when some foul storm's on its way."

"A wonderful ability," she said. "I would imagine being able to predict difficult weather would come in quite handy."

"Yes, ma'am," Gideon said, tugging on his knit cap. "Has sure been a blessing on occasion."

Although Drew had already pulled on his gloves and was waiting at the door, Gideon strode over to Sara. Then he gathered her in his arms, gave her a bear hug, and turned her loose. "Thanks for supper, Sara. We'll return the favor soon."

Her gaze searched his before a hesitant smile curved her mouth. "You're welcome, Gideon. I look forward to seeing your home."

On that, Gideon and Drew ventured out into the cold, making Caleb hurry to the door to try to kick out the snow that had blown in despite the fact the door hadn't been open long.

"Oh my," Sara said. She grabbed the broom and swept up a pile of the thick snow. She glanced to Caleb. "Should I sweep this outside?"

He shook his head. "It'll only blow right back in and bring more with it." Crouching, he scooped the snow in his hands and started packing it into a ball. "S'pose we could bundle up, head outside, and have ourselves a fight. Ain't dark with all the snow and the full moon."

"I beg your pardon?"

"It's a full moon right now and—"

"I was referring to your discussion of us quarreling."

He grinned. "We wouldn't argue, honey. I meant a *snowball* fight. Ain't you never had a snowball fight?" He held up his fresh snowball.

She wrinkled her brow. "Are you telling me you would dare to hurl that at me?"

"Well, yeah... It's fun, Sara. I wouldn't hurt you none. I swear."

"I fear I'm having a difficult time seeing how it would be amusing to toss a bundle of ice at anyone, let alone my husband."

Had she been a man, he'd have thrown it at her right then and there just to show her how to start a rousing snowball fight, but he wasn't entirely sure she'd appreciate his offbeat sense of humor. Instead, he bent down and tossed the melting snowball into the stove, listening to the hiss and watching steam rise.

The sudden cold on his neck made him snap up. His hand shot to the cold skin, finding some melted snow that he swept aside. "What the hell?"

Sara was nibbling on her bottom lip, her fingers wet from the snow she'd plopped on him.

"Why, Mrs. Young... Are you perhaps teasin' me?"

She nodded, still tugging at her bottom lip. He wasn't sure if she was nervous and fearing she'd overstepped her bounds or trying to stifle a giggle.

"Then get ready for my revenge." Hoping she'd see the fun in what he was about to do, he growled and charged. Dropping his shoulder, he grabbed her backside, lifting her. He arranged her like a sack of grain over his shoulder and headed for the door. "I reckon the best revenge is to give you your bath in a snow drift tonight."

With a squeal, she slapped her hands against his back. "You wouldn't dare!" Then she laughed, making him smile.

Caleb jerked the door open and strode out into the snow. It still fell heavily as he marched to the pile he'd made when he'd cleared the walkway to the house earlier in the day. He stopped and feigned flipping her into it.

Sara's fingers dug into his flannel shirt as she tried to stay on his shoulder. "Caleb! No!"

"No?" He smacked her backside. "You started this. I'm only payin' you back in kind."

She squirmed against him. "I'm sorry. I thought you'd find it amusing."

"I did," he admitted.

Her gasp echoed around them. "And you still think to toss me into the snow?"

Easing her from his shoulder, Caleb set her on her feet. When he noticed she was shivering, he took her into his arms and settled his mouth on hers.

There was something different in her kiss, a wealth of emotion that had been absent before. She was the first to deepen the exchange, slipping her tongue into his mouth and lazily rubbing it across his.

Despite the cold, he'd have been content to stand there all night. But Sara trembled, and while he hoped it was from passion inspired by the kiss, he wasn't about to make that assumption. He broke away and swept her into his arms. "Fun's over for now. Need to get you warm again."

Back inside the house, he brushed the snow from her hair and shoulders. Damn, but she was a beautiful woman. Her cheeks were rosy from the cold, and her eyes sparkled as she smiled up at him in a way that made his cock harden.

Sara could see Caleb's confusion. Not only was it plain in his eyes, but as he stared at her, he'd tilted his head like a curious child.

She'd come to an important decision.

It was time to allow her husband to truly share her bed.

He'd been so kind, so gentle. He'd shown her pleasure that she'd never dreamed possible, but it cost him. Not that he was rude to her or took out his sexual frustration on her. No, he was almost too kind, too solicitous.

Yet she could feel the depth of his desire. He was a passionate man, and he deserved a true wife, one who gave him everything she had to give. She was so very lucky to have him as her savior, and she was ready to offer him her body freely. In all honesty, she wanted to see if the delights he'd shown her with his fingers and his mouth would be half as sweet when he claimed her with his body.

The bad memories were fading more and more with each passing day in Caleb's company. Her nightmares had ended. Having him hold her close through the long, chilly nights kept her demons at bay, and Sara dared to hope the past would stay in the past.

While on the road to accepting Caleb, she'd also achieved a peace she'd never expected. She'd begun to forgive herself. She no longer thought of herself as a whore, nor did she constantly berate herself for having been forced into working at The Palace. The only taint preventing her from assigning her past to nothing but harmless memories was the anger. She couldn't seem to shed her hatred for Jean-Claude setting her in Crazy Kate's control.

Perhaps one day...

For now, Sara wanted to explore her growing feelings for Caleb and to make a good life for them on this wonderful farm. Their marriage was the most important thing in her life, and the time had come to accept her husband as her lover.

Rising on tiptoes, she stretched her arms around his neck and kissed him again. Their tongues lazily mated, a thrust and parry that sent her head spinning. When they finally ended the kiss, she was thrilled he was panting for breath. To her surprise, she was as well.

"Need to get outta those wet clothes, sweetheart," he said, smoothing his knuckles against her cheek.

"So should you," she said. She grasped the top button of his shirt and opened it. Then she popped the second.

"What are you doin'?"

"I'm helping you get out of this wet shirt." She opened two more buttons.

Caleb pressed her hands flat against his stomach. "Sara... Honey, you go change first. Get out of them wet clothes, put on a warm nightgown, and get in bed. I'll join you in the bedroom soon."

Sara fisted his loose shirt in her hands and tugged. "How about you join me in the bedroom *now?*"

He groaned as he dropped his chin to his chest.

She nudged his face back up so she could see his eyes. "I am quite serious, husband. I–I am...ready. Ready for more than sleeping at your side."

His gaze searched hers and his fingers dug into her hips. "Ready? Sara, are you sayin'—" He breathed a sigh and shook his head.

"Am I saying what, Caleb?"

"Sara, it ain't right to tease a man. Not about...that. I want you too much to stand it."

"I assure you that I am not teasing you." She pulled her arms back, took his hand in hers, and led him to the bedroom door. "And I want you too. I want to be your wife in every way."

"You're sure?"

"I want you, Caleb."

Caleb's mouth was on hers as he embraced her. His tongue thrust into her mouth while his hands rubbed her back, moving slowly lower.

Heat bloomed between her thighs. By giving her time and showing her the way he could make her body sing, her husband had done more than teach her to trust him. He'd freed a part of her that she'd never known before—the passionate Sara who now yearned for his touch.

His hands settled on her backside, pulling her hard against his groin. She wiggled against him, no longer dreading the feel of an erection. Instead, knowing she'd pulled that reaction from his body made her heart pound and her blood run hot.

Sara wriggled her hands between them, tugging his shirt from the waist of his pants, needing to touch him, to feel his skin beneath her fingertips.

As she tried to strip his clothes, he returned the favor, tugging her blouse apart so roughly, the pearl buttons popped off, skittering across the floor.

A loud pounding at the door interrupted their interlude.

Sara froze, fear snaking through her like ice water in her veins. No one had ever come calling without an invitation, and someone arriving so late could only be bad news. "Gideon, perhaps?" she whispered, struggling for an explanation.

Turning her loose, Caleb strode to the door as he stuffed his shirt back into his waistband. He grabbed the rifle he always left propped behind the coat tree. "Who's there?"

Someone shouted an answer, but she couldn't hear from so far away. She busied herself with trying to right her blouse, a difficult task considering she'd lost several of the buttons.

Caleb opened the door, sending snow swirling inside as a man stepped through, too bundled up in a knit scarf and hat for her to identify.

"Damn, Adam," Caleb said. "You're gonna freeze to death."

Adam. This had to be Adam Morgan, a man Caleb had told her a lot about. The stories showed how much her husband admired the older man, and she worried that she'd be meeting someone so important to Caleb in such disheveled clothing.

She tried to scurry inside the bedroom, hoping to quickly change her blouse, but a shout stopped her. "Wait!"

"Sir?" she asked, whirling to face him as her skirts swished around her ankles.

He started unwrapping the scarf, revealing a kind face ruddy from the cold. "Are you Sara?"

"I am."

"Sara," Caleb said, taking the scarf from Adam. "This is Adam Morgan."

She inclined her head. "It is my pleasure to meet you, Mr. Morgan."

"Adam," he said, plucking the thick knit cap from his head. His short hair stood on end, but she suppressed a smile at him being every bit as unkempt as she was. "Please."

Clutching at the front of her blouse so it wouldn't gape open, she hurried to Caleb's side. "Might we inquire what has brought you to our home in such foul weather?" she asked, glad that the hard pounding of her heart had begun to ease. She was quite confident there was nothing to fear from Adam Morgan—at least according to her husband.

She trusted Caleb.

Completely.

Although she should've been amazed or at least perplexed by that startling revelation, Sara simply gave her head a little shake. Now wasn't the time to ponder such a momentous change, nor was she willing to explore what tender feelings might lie beneath that trust.

"Ty sent me," Adam replied. He moved to the fire, warming his hands by rubbing them together.

"Why on earth would Ty send you here?" Caleb asked. He draped Adam's scarf over a chair. "Especially on a night like this? The snow's pilling up out there."

Adam snorted. "Wasn't a pleasant ride. That's for damned sure."

Her curiosity was killing her. "Then why—"

"Cassie," he interrupted. "I came because of Cassie."

That made no sense. Unless...

Her heart started slamming in her chest again as fear flooded her. "Has she become ill?" She put her hand on Caleb's chest. "If she's ill, I should go to her."

Adam shook his head. "Cassie's not ill, Sara. It's her time. She's taken to her childbed, and she begged me to fetch you to be with her when the baby comes."

Chapter Eleven

Sara's hands were so cold, she could barely open the door to Ty's home. She shivered so hard her teeth chattered, and she longed to strip her coat, hat, scarf, and mittens and warm herself in front of a roaring fire.

"Cassie?" she called as she stepped inside.

"She's in here!" Ty came stomping out of the bedroom. He set his hands against his hips and glared at her. "Took you long enough!"

Since it was next to impossible to have conversation with her face wrapped tight, Sara unwound the scarf, not surprised to find it caked with ice and snow.

The weather fought them the whole way. Adam had hitched his horse to a small sleigh to get them through the storm. Between the high winds and drifting snow, the ride had been treacherous. Had the trip been for a less important reason, Sara would have stayed home. But how could she refuse her new sister by marriage? Thankfully, Adam seemed adept at handling the horse and got them to their destination safely.

Now Sara understood why people from Montana tended to believe they were such sturdy folk. Rough winters had a way of making people strong.

Caleb remained behind to care for the animals, promising to follow in the morning to see how things were going. After the horrible trip through nearly blinding snow, Sara wished she had some way to contact her husband to tell him to stay home where he was safe and warm. Perhaps when he saw that the weather had taken a turn for the worse he'd reconsider. She had enough on her mind at the moment and hated to add worry for Caleb's safety.

Her brother continued to glare at her as she removed her mittens and coat and set them on the back of a chair near the stove so they could dry. "We came as quickly as we could manage," she said, rubbing her hands together. The stinging feel of the skin rewarming made her wince.

Ty grabbed her elbow and tugged her toward the bedroom. "Cassie needs you. Now."

Sara had never seen her brother so rattled. Ty had always been a man who could hold his countenance. It took a lot to get him angry, but then his temper burned hot and fierce.

But fear?

That was new to her. Although he was dragging her like a naughty child about to be disciplined, she had to smile. Her brother obviously loved Cassie a great deal. Only his wife could throw Ty off center so effectively.

Cassie was on the bed, red-faced and panting for air. Sitting on the side of the bed was a woman who had one hand on Cassie's swollen abdomen.

"It's easing now," the woman said, her voice soft yet full of confidence. "Rest until the next one comes on you. The pains are still a bit apart, so we might have a long night ahead of us."

"Sara," Cassie said, still a bit breathless. "You came."

Ty gave Sara a nudge into the room. "Told you she'd come." He went to the opposite side of the bed, sat down, and took Cassie's hand in his. "Told you so," he said again with a decisive nod.

With a wan smile, Cassie nodded in return. Then she closed her eyes and dropped her head against the pillows piled up behind her. "I'm sorry I can't greet you properly, Sara."

"Oh, pish-posh," Sara said, coming closer. "You're far too busy for pleasantries."

The woman chuckled. She picked up a small cloth, dipped it in the pan of water, and wrung it out before laying it across Cassie's forehead. Her gaze shifted to Sara. "You must be Sara Young."

"Yes, ma'am."

"I'm Grace Morgan. I'm pleased to finally meet you. Ty has told us so much about you."

Sara froze. Surely Ty had protected her secret. The welcome she saw in Grace's eyes had to mean that she saw Sara as nothing more than Ty's sister or Caleb's wife. "I–I'm pleased to meet you as well."

"Are you settling in on Caleb's farm?"

"Yes, ma'am."

"You can call me Grace. I imagine helping Cassie through the birth of her child should suspend any formalities." Her smile was welcoming. Dressed in a tan blouse—the sleeves rolled up to the elbow—and a brown skirt, she fussed over Cassie. "We're here to help Cassie bring her baby into the world. She told me she really wanted to have her new sister at her side. It was good of you to brave the cold to come to her."

"Of course I came. It was very kind of your husband to come out in this storm to fetch me, although I'm afraid I can offer nothing but moral support," Sara admitted. "I have never attended a birth before."

"I still think I should go for Doc Adams," Ty insisted before kissing the back of Cassie's hand. "I'm worried 'bout you, Cassie girl."

Without even opening her eyes, Cassie shook her head. "We talked about this already, Ty. I'm fine. Grace has had two children, and I have Sara to hold my hand."

"But—"

"I don't want Doc Adams," Cassie insisted. "I'm—" Her words
ended on a grunt as she lifted her head from the pillow and squeezed
her eyes shut.

Grace's hand flew to Cassie's abdomen. "Breathe through the pain,
honey. They're starting to come closer now, aren't they?" She kept up
pleasant chatter, probably trying to distract the expectant mother.

Not sure how to help, Sara went to where Ty sat at Cassie's side.
His face contorted as though he was in pain as well. "Ty? Are you ill?"
Sara asked.

"She's gonna break my hand," he whispered, nodding toward
where Cassie had a tight grip on him.

"Almost there, Cassie," Grace said. "It's easing, isn't it?"

Cassie nodded but still bit hard at her bottom lip.

Sara's heart went out to her, and she offered up a quick prayer that
mother and baby come through the birth healthy. Cassie was so little.
How could such a small woman bring a baby into the world?

"Ty," Grace said, her voice calm as she took the cloth and
refreshed it in the pan of water. "I think you should go and wait with
Adam. I'm sure he'd welcome some brandy, and I imagine you could
use some as well."

"More like whiskey," he snapped. Cassie had let go of his hand,
and he shook it as if to return the circulation. "But I can't leave
Cassie."

"Yes," Grace countered, "you can. It's time for you to take your
leave. Let us take care of Cassie."

"But—"

Cassie cut him off with a curt order as she pointed at the door.
"Go. Now."

His gaze shifted from Cassie to Grace to Sara and back to Cassie.
"Are you sure, Cassie girl?"

"Go. Now."

Dragging his feet like a child being ordered to do his chores, Ty
took his time following his wife's command. At the door, he cast one
more glance to his wife.

"Go on." Grace shooed him away with a flip of her hand. "This is
no place for a man."

He closed the door behind him.

At loss for how to help, Sara took the place next to Cassie that Ty
had vacated. "Why did you wish him to leave?"

Grace smoothed the wet cloth over Cassie's face. "This is no place
for a man," she said again.

Cassie snorted. "I don't want him seeing me like...like...*this*. In
pain? Laid out on this bed like a fileted haddock? No thanks."

Sara couldn't help but chuckle at the imagery. "I suppose it is a bit...ignoble."

"A fitting word," Grace said. "Men don't understand. They can't deal with the pain. Or the blood."

When Cassie clutched for her hand, Sara took it and stroked Cassie's palm with her thumb. "But they aren't the one in pain. What is there to handle?"

"Of course they're not," Grace replied. "Not only could men not tolerate the kind of pain childbirth brings, they cannot handle seeing a woman hurting so, nor can they deal with the rather messy side of having a baby."

"D–does it hurt badly?" Sara asked. Her curiosity was tainted with her fear. Although she knew a bit of how a child came into the world, she'd never quite accepted exactly how the child made his way from his mother's body. The notion of a child's head emerging from...*there? Impossible.*

"It's hard to describe." Cassie relaxed against the pillows again. "But it's no picnic."

Grace smoothed her fingers across Cassie's cheek. "As soon as you hold your son in your arms—"

"I'm having a daughter," Cassie announced. "And I'll hear no arguments against it."

After a chuckle, Grace said, "Your daughter, then. When you're holding her in your arms, the pain will be all but forgotten."

***

Caleb was grateful the snow had stopped. Sunrise was still a good hour away, but he was bundled up and half way through the trek to Ty's home.

He was proud of Sara for braving the cold and drifting snow to be with Cassie in her time of need. Although he'd always wanted a family, he'd never considered how difficult it was for a woman to bring a child into the world. Cassie was facing a trial, but Sara would be with her.

Since Adam had come to fetch her, Caleb assumed Grace Morgan was there as well. A good thing considering he had no idea if Sara had any experience with helping a woman deliver a baby.

Would Cassie and Grace come to help Sara when her time came? Not that he expected to become a father any time soon. He'd only made love to his wife once. But the future boded well—especially for tonight. Sara had given him exactly what he'd worked so hard to earn.

Her trust.

She'd wanted to share his bed for more than sleeping or him

pleasuring her, and he'd felt the hunger in her kiss, the desire in her touch. From today forward, they would be in a true marriage—one of both companionship and passion.

How long would it take Cassie to have her baby? A few hours, more or less? The baby didn't have too awfully far to travel.

He gave his head a shake to rid himself of the image of a baby being forced from a woman's body.

How could mother and child survive such an ordeal? It was a miracle anyone was ever born at all.

His only experience with birth was attending sheep and horses. Those females handled birth with very little fuss and bother. Surely a human giving birth wouldn't have any more trouble than a mare or a ewe. Perhaps his overactive imagination was exaggerating how difficult a human birth was since he'd never seen one.

Caleb guided the one-horse sleigh around another rather large snowdrift, grateful to see the Bishop's home in the distance—nothing but a dark spot surrounded by pines set in a field of white. While it might have been faster to ride, he still had no idea if Sara could handle a horse. They'd only been together six weeks. She'd never had the to opportunity to show whether she was able to handle a horse well enough for long distances. The few places they'd traveled by horseback, they hadn't ventured far from home. A frigid winter morning was no time to put her new abilities to the test.

He'd helped Sara bundle up for the trip and hoped she'd made it with little discomfort. It was colder now, something that tended to happen right after a good snowfall. Caleb had planned for his trip well, dressing in layers and covering almost all of his exposed skin. He'd also grabbed some wolf pelts to help make the trip home more comfortable for his wife.

And once they got back home, he'd stoke a fire inside her that would banish the cold for both of them.

The trip normally took about an hour. Even though he couldn't check his pocket watch, Caleb knew almost two had passed. The sun was rising, although no warmth came with it. By the time he reached Ty's home, he was cold, tired, and cranky. He'd give himself some time to warm up before he scooped up Sara, got her wrapped nice and warm, and then got her home. Where she belonged.

Adam came from the house, probably alerted by the sleigh's bells. He'd donned his coat and gloves and was pulling a knit cap over his head. He grabbed the horse's bridle and held the animal steady while Caleb climbed out of the sleigh. "Didn't expect to see you so early."

"Early?" He helped Adam unhitch the sleigh and set it aside as Adam led the horse toward the barn. "It's a good hour after dawn.

Figured the baby arrived hours ago. Thought I'd let Sara rest up before taking her home."

"Rest up?" Adam's chuckle rose from his mouth in white clouds. "I'm guessing you've never waited for a woman giving birth before."

"Of course not," Caleb said. "But seen plenty of ewes and mares and—"

Adam let out a deeper chuckle. "Let me give you a bit of advice, son. I wouldn't be likening the women to sheep or horses. Doubt they'd take too kindly to the comparison."

After the horse was rubbed down and put in a stall, Caleb followed Adam into the house. Ty didn't even acknowledge them, pacing from one side of the room to another. None of the women were anywhere to be seen.

A scream rent the air, making all the men stop and turn to stare at the bedroom door. A cold chill ran the length of Caleb's spine at hearing Cassie's voice in such obvious pain.

When Ty sprinted for the door, Adam blocked his path. "Wait."

"Get outta my way Adam." Ty clenched his hands at his sides.

"You're not going in there until—"

Another sound, a baby's lusty cry, spilled from the bedroom.

"See?" Adam said, cuffing Ty on the shoulder. "All's well. Let Grace and Sara help Cassie get settled. She won't want you to see her 'til she's ready."

"Sara!" Ty shouted. "Is Cassie all right?"

"She's fine," came Sara's muffled reply. "So is the baby."

A grin spread over Adam's face. "Our Sara is such a clever girl."

"Clever?" Caleb asked. "Don't get me wrong, I think Sara's clever too. Just not sure what made you mention it now."

"Did you happen to notice," Adam replied, "that she didn't mention whether that rather loud baby is a boy or a girl? She's going to let Cassie share the happy news with Ty."

Chapter Twelve

Sara cradled the newborn, marveling at the ten tiny fingers and chubby pink face. The baby's eyelashes were thick and brown, and her fingernails were delicate and long enough to need trimming.

Such a miracle. So perfectly formed. So small. So very...loud.

After pitching a crying fit after her birth, the little girl settled down until Sara bathed her. The water—even though it was warm—had set the child to bellowing, so Sara hurried, being sure to clean away the messy part of bringing a child into the world while Grace tended to Cassie.

The night had been long and, for Sara, filled with worry. Cassie was brave, bearing up as wave after wave of pains assailed her. Toward the end, she'd pulled her knees up and pushed hard enough her face flushed cherry-red. Had Grace not been there, Sara would have panicked, worried that the baby was stuck or that it wasn't in the proper position for birthing.

But Grace had been every bit the embodiment of her name. She'd told Cassie about the two times she'd given birth and had offered encouragement. To distract the expectant mother, Grace had kept up a stream of chatter, asking questions of both Cassie and Sara and fussing with tasks like refolding already orderly towels or dusting the pristine furniture. Sara quickly learned that whenever Cassie was distracted, she seemed better able to handle her labors, so Sara had joined in, trying to learn more about her brother and her husband and see them through Cassie's eyes.

When the baby's birth drew near, the normally sweet-natured Cassie had morphed into an angry shrew, even bellowing profanities at Ty through the closed door. Ty had shouted back an apology, no matter what it was that Cassie blamed him for—everything from causing her to be in her predicament to bringing about the snow storm that had kept the wind crying through the night.

Grace smoothed the clean quilt over Cassie. "Now remember...take it easy. Daisy will be coming to help so I can get some rest, but I'll be back soon. You've just fought a war and need to let your body recover."

"I shall remember," Cassie replied. "Truth be told, I'm far too weary and sore to do anything except hold my daughter." She beckoned to Sara.

Sara smiled and settled the baby in Cassie's arms.

Cassie stroked one tiny palm with her pinkie, causing the baby to grasp and hold that finger tightly.

"Thank you both," Cassie said, tears filling her eyes. "I will never be able to tell you how much it meant to me to have you both here. I could never have survived had you not come to my aid. I panic when I ponder Ty performing those duties. I never wish for him to see me in such an dreadful position."

"I think of you as my own daughter." Tears pooled in Grace's eyes as well. "Just as Ty is my son. I'm honored you asked for me to attend you."

"And you, Sara." Cassie sniffed. "You are the sister I always wished for, and I hope you will stand as godmother for my child."

Although Sara had grown up with Jacqueline, she'd never once considered her "charge" as sisterly. Jacqueline treated Sara as a servant. Sara's own sisters had all abandoned her to life, as had her brothers.

Except Ty.

Ty had been the one to relentlessly track her down. Had he not done so, she'd still be at The Palace, playing the whore for men not worthy to spit upon. But thanks to her brother, she had a loving husband and a home of her own.

Godmother? Never in her life would Sara have believed someone would ask her to perform that sacred duty.

And now she had a sister who cared for her.

Tears spilling down her cheeks, Sara could only nod.

"Now you must give my daughter a cousin—someone she can grow up with," Cassie ordered. "You and Caleb must start a family of your own."

The sincerity and love in Cassie's voice made Sara long to immediately agree. But she wasn't sure she could ever be a mother. Instead of replying with the stark truth, she only nodded again. There was no need tainting such a beautiful moment with sadness. The burden was Sara's alone to bear.

Grace smoothed the backs of her hands over her cheeks. "Just look at the three of us weeping. The men are likely to see us and think there's a problem."

A loud knock sounded. "Everything okay in there? Ain't hearing cryin' no more." Ty shouted through the door. The incessant rattle of the knob spoke of his urgency to meet his new child and see to his wife's welfare.

"You may come in," Cassie called.

Sara and Grace stepped back, a good thing considering Ty— followed closely by Caleb and Adam—spilled into the room. Taking a seat on the side of the bed, Ty gently touched his daughter's head with a trembling hand.

"We have a daughter," Cassie said. "A fine healthy daughter."

Ty smoothed his hand over the baby's brown hair, making it lie flat. The tresses immediately stood back on end. "Why's it do that?" he asked, his tone full of wonder.

"Pardon?" Cassie asked, knitting her brows. "What does what do what?"

"Her hair," Ty replied. "It stands on end like something gave her an awful scare."

While everyone chuckled, Cassie frowned. "Her hair is beautiful." She kissed the baby's head.

Ty kissed Cassie's forehead. "You did good, Cassie girl."

"*We* did *well*," she countered.

Caleb came to stand by Sara and snaked an arm around her waist. She was so worn-out she leaned heavily against him and yawned.

"You tired, sweetheart?" he asked.

She let out another yawn as she nodded. "A rather unnecessary question considering it's past dawn."

"Do you have a name picked out for my granddaughter?" Adam asked. He stepped behind his wife and wrapped his arms around her. She closed her eyes and leaned back against him, clearly as exhausted as Sara was.

Sara was so weary Adam's question made little sense. "Granddaughter? How can she be your—?" Ty's story of how Adam had taken him and Jake Curtis in and raised them as his own sons came flooding back. "Oh. Pardon my confusion."

If only someone as kind as Adam Morgan had taken her in as a child, her future would have been so very different. Instead she'd become an indentured servant and then an inexperienced mistress to a man who'd used her and then sold her into Crazy Kate's service.

But there was no use wishing for what could never be.

Thankfully, Adam's smile spoke of forgiveness.

"We ain't talked about names," Ty replied. "Guess we've got a chore to do."

A soft chuckle from Cassie was interrupted by a yawn, and the heaviness of her eyelids attested to how hard the new mother struggled to stay awake.

"Well then...I'd say you two have plenty to discuss." Adam rubbed his wife's shoulders. "Snow's let up, Gracie. Let me take you home. You need some rest."

"I need to see Benjamin first," she said. "Then I can sleep."

"Benjamin?" Sara asked.

"Our son," Adam replied.

"He's three," Grace added. "Cassie?"

Cassie glanced up from her daughter.

"I'll be back soon," Grace promised. "Daisy was supposed to set out at dawn. She should be here anytime."

Cassie nodded.

"Don't you worry none," a friendly rather husky woman's voice sang from the other room. "Daisy's here!"

With the force of a tornado, a plump, gray-haired woman rushed into the bedroom. She hurried to the bed. "Yes, ma'am. I'll take right good care of Miss Cassie and this beautiful new baby."

"I have a daughter, Daisy," Cassie said.

The familiarity was evident, so Sara didn't ask who this whirlwind was.

"Daisy keeps the Morgans' house," Caleb whispered in her ear. "But she's more like family."

She gave him a quick nod of understanding, grateful he'd so easily followed her thought process. "Shall we go home? If the snow has stopped, will the trip be treacherous?"

"The sun's coming out good and strong," Caleb replied. "It'll be warm enough to melt some of the snow away. I'd be happy to take you home."

***

Will I ever be warm again?

Although Caleb had gone to considerable effort to make the trip home as cozy as possible, Sara felt chilled to the bone. She shed her outer garments and huddled close to the heat. Thankfully, he'd lit a fire in the stove and in the bedroom hearth before going out to tend the horses, but even the rising flames couldn't seem to help her banish the cold.

Shivering hard enough her teeth chattered, she rubbed her hands together, hating the stinging feeling of them rewarming almost as much as she'd hated them feeling like blocks of ice. A moan slipped out as she shifted her weight between her numb feet to try to restore circulation.

Sara flopped into a chair and tried to remove her boots. Her fingers were too stiff to obey her will. She probably should have alerted her husband to her growing discomfort on the ride home, but he'd been preoccupied simply guiding the horses along the barely visible path he'd made in the snow on his trip to Ty's house. Since he had to be suffering from the cold every bit as much as she'd been, she wasn't about to complain.

Now she was paying the price. She knew little of how to help frostbite, and all she could think to do was get her shoes and socks off, move close to the fire, and hope there was no permanent damage. Her fingers were turning red as they rewarmed, something she hoped was a good sign. Unfortunately, they were also beginning to swell, looking more and more like fat sausages.

Just when she'd abandoned hope of getting her boots off, Caleb came in, shaking the snow off his coat. He took one look at where she'd left her coat, mittens, hat, and scarf on the floor and frowned.

"I'm sorry to be so untidy," Sara said through teeth that still chattered. "I–I wanted to get close to the fire."

He shook his head. "Don't rightly care about that. Are you all right?"

"F–fine." A shudder raced through her body. "I seem to be having trouble sh–shaking the chill."

Caleb jerked off his hat, scarf, and gloves, dropping them on top of her small pile. His coat quickly followed. He strode across the room to kneel in front of her, taking her hands in his.

How could his hands be so warm after that long, cold ride and then tending to the horses?

He turned her hands over so he could look at her palms. "You're near to frostbit, sweetheart. Why didn't you tell me you were hurtin'?"

Sara shrugged.

Rubbing her hands with his own, he helped the circulation return. With it came more of the pain that felt like dozens if not hundreds of pin pricks. She bit her lip hard to keep from moaning, but tears pooled in her eyes. She dropped her chin so he wouldn't notice.

"What about your feet?" he asked. He finally let her hands go. "They hurtin' too?" It only took him a few moments to remove her boots and socks.

Her feet were white.

"Oh, Sara. Sweetheart, we gotta get you warm." Caleb stood and scooped her into his arms. Instead of carrying her closer to the stove, he strode to their bedroom. "Need to get you out of them wet clothes and wrapped up with something warm."

She didn't fight him when he unbuttoned her shirt. Since his intent was solely focused on helping get her warm, she saw no need to fight him. If anything, she took great comfort in knowing he was concerned for her wellbeing.

Trust. She truly did trust him. Once she was warm, she intended to follow through with the promise she'd made. She would be his wife in truth, and her body shook at the notion that the pleasure he'd shown her would not only continue but grow when they shared themselves with each other. Funny, but her passionate thoughts were helping relieve the chill.

In no time, he had her stripped even her underwear, but he quickly covered her with a flannel nightgown. He swept the covers aside, picked her up, and set her on the mattress.

"What is warm enough to wrap me up in?"

"Me." With a glint in his eyes, he stripped quickly, coming to the bed naked. And aroused.

Caleb hadn't forgotten her promise and her declaration of desire. Hell, his cock got hard the moment he'd stepped back in their house. He wasn't going to push her, though. Right now she needed his warmth. Only when she was again comfortable would he try for more.

He lay back on the mattress and rolled her on top on him so her front pressed against his. He tucked her head under his chin. "Jesus have mercy!"

"What's wrong?"

"You're as cold as an icicle." Opening his legs, he let hers settle between. Squeezing his thighs together, he tried to draw away her cold. He jerked the blankets over them and then wrapped his arms around her.

Sara's shivering eased and then disappeared. She nuzzled her face against his neck, her sweet, warm breaths brushing against his skin and heating his blood. Her breasts were flattened against his chest, and her nipples were hard pebbles, branding his skin. The only thing between them was her thin nightgown, and he wished he'd have removed that as well.

He deliberately left her nightgown alone because he needed to give her the choice. While he wanted desperately to make love to her, a few hours after she'd just witnessed a birth might not be the right time. After he'd watched a cowboy bust his collarbone breaking a horse, he'd avoided that task for a good long while.

Hopefully Sara wouldn't refuse his bed because she feared childbirth. Caleb wanted a family, and now was as good a time to start one as any. There was affection between him and his wife. Not love. Not quite yet. But he trusted her as she now trusted him, and that was a better start than many marriages enjoyed.

He nuzzled his nose against her hair, loving the soft, silky feel. Despite having been up all night tending Cassie Bishop, Sara still bore her clean and appealing scent. As her body warmed, so did his, and he was more than aware that her pelvis lay against his. His cock was stiff as granite, and his mind whirled with pictures of the erotic things he wanted to do with her.

"I owe you an apology," he murmured, gently stroking her backside.

Sara eased back, staring up at him with knit brows. "An apology?"

"Our wedding night was a disaster."

"You already apologized for that, Caleb."

"I wasn't much of a lover," he admitted.

"I believe you have striven to prove that you *are*," she murmured before her lips brushed against his neck. "You have given me great pleasure, the likes of which I had never known."

His cock twitched. "So you'll let me make love to you?"

"No," she replied. "Not this time."

"What's that mean?"

Sara pushed herself up, her breasts drilling his chest as her gaze found his in the faint light of the fire. Her eyes sparkled as a slow, easy smile curved her mouth. "What that means is that this time, *I* shall make love to *you*."

Chapter Thirteen

Caleb gaped up at his wife. She'd risen to straddle his hips, and her hot, wet core nestled against his hard cock. Such exquisite torture. It would be so simple to thrust inside her, but her words haunted him and kept him from moving.

"I shall make love to you."

Sara nibbled on her bottom lip as she eased her nightgown up. With a deep breath, she jerked it over her head and let it fall to the floor.

She was exquisite. Firm breasts crowned with nipples that had hardened in invitation. He settled his palms against those breasts, rubbing and weighing each. As Sara unplaited her hair, Caleb sat up and drew one of the pink nubs into his mouth.

With a loud gasp, she arched into him, lacing her fingers through his hair as he suckled, licked, and teased her breast. A hum rose from her, much like a cat purring, which made him shift to her other breast to worship it as well.

After long moments, she put her hands against his shoulders and pushed. "I am supposed to be making love to you. Lie back and let me. Please."

Although he was content to lavish her with attention, Caleb gave in to her command. His curiosity was running as fast as a spooked deer, and he wanted to see exactly how she'd launch her attack.

She seemed to be considering the same thing, concentrating hard before her teeth tugged on her bottom lip again.

Afraid she'd gone craven he offered her a chance to back out—even though it would be the biggest disappointment of his life if she stopped. "Change your mind, sweetheart?"

She gave her head a shake, setting her hair bouncing around her shoulders. "Planning my first move."

Leaning forward, she cupped his face in her hands and kissed him, long and deep. Her tongue pushed past his lips and rubbed against his tongue, sending more heat pouring through his body.

His beautiful wife was truly going to make love to him.

Caleb smiled against her lips.

Sara had come close to losing her courage. The cold seemed to never want to leave, but once her body warmed, so did her heart. Caleb had taken such infinite care to help her banish her chill, and the way his eyes glowed with passion when he saw her naked had helped her find what little valor she possessed.

She hadn't fibbed when she told her husband she wanted him. Desire was so new to her, and it was Caleb who'd awakened her body, almost as though she'd been a virgin in her feelings if not in truth.

Her entire body responded to his touch the way it had to no other. A few of the men she'd been with had tried to coax her into passion, but none had achieved that goal. The other girls had taught her to act out such a response, telling her men often paid more if they believed themselves to be good lovers. Thinking their whore had found fulfillment evidently made them feel virile and manly.

She shoved aside any more thoughts of her past and concentrated on her future.

Caleb responded to her kisses with enthusiasm and a touch of desperation. Sara eased back, letting her hands run down his chest and tickling her fingers in the patch of dark hair covering his chest. She traced the line of hair as it narrowed, circling his navel with her finger, and stopped short of touching his erection.

For once, she admired the beauty in a man's body. Caleb's cock was hard, arrogant, ready. Knowing that she'd pulled that reaction from his body through affection rather than lust made her smile as she wrapped her fingers around his shaft.

"Sara... You ain't got to—"

She shook her head. "Hush, husband. Let me show you how I..." She swallowed hard. "How I feel about you."

A couple of seconds ticked by as she contemplated what she'd had to stop herself from saying.

Let me show you how I love you...

Love?

Did she *love* her husband?

Giving her head another shake, she banished any thought other than sharing herself with Caleb. Sara eased to his side, kneeling next to him as she stroked his erection. His breathing sped, his hips rising to each caress. Happy he was enjoying her attention, she took a leap of faith, choosing to gift her husband with something she'd never done for any other man, no matter how much money many of them had offered for the act.

She took the head of his cock in her mouth, letting herself drown in his salty taste and musky scent.

He almost came off the bed. "Sara...You ain't got to..." His fingers threaded through her hair when she swallowed most of his considerable length. "Don't stop!"

Being in control, gifting her attentions rather than having them demanded, made all the difference in the world. She meant something to this man, this wonderful man who offered her his affection, his fidelity, and—God willing—someday his love.

Her core throbbed in need, and with her feelings so entwined with her passion, Sara was close to losing control. She released him and again straddled his hips. One long, deep kiss before she gripped his cock, guided it to her sheath, and closed her eyes as she waited for him to thrust inside her.

After a moment passed and he didn't move, she opened her eyes.

He stared up at her, a perplexed expression on his face.

"What's wrong, Caleb?"

"I want you," he said in a husky murmur.

"As I want you."

"Then take me inside you, Sara. Show me you want me."

His request sent her heart soaring. He was giving her exactly what she needed—control over her own body.

She pressed down, impaling herself on him, letting him fill her. Completely.

Caleb's hands held her hips as he guided Sara in a rhythm that soon had the tension building to a crescendo. Music—a symphony she'd once attended—captured her mind, the volume and speed of the opus increasing as her body tightened with each note, each thrust of his body into hers.

Never had she imagined she would enjoy mating. He'd healed her, offered her a sparkling new life as though the old Sara Fuller never existed. In the moment where she found her fulfillment, where she believed their hearts beat as one, she gave her heart and soul to her savior—Caleb Young.

Caleb groaned his wife's name as he climaxed, pouring his seed deep inside Sara. He shuddered, clenching her hips and thrusting into her even after the storm had passed. Never had he experienced the type of satisfaction that thrummed through him at that moment. He wanted to stay inside her forever, to stay joined with her body and remain one flesh.

He'd always known having a wife would be a blessing in his lonely life, but he hadn't expected anything nearly as wonderful as what he shared with Sara. She was more than a mere wife.

She was his mate—his other half.

What they'd just shared, the way he'd felt as he'd touched her womb, told him that God had truly blessed him by sending him not only a *good* wife but the *right* one.

Breaking their connection, Sara rolled away. Caleb tossed the quilt over them, wrapped an arm around her shoulder, and hauled her up against his side.

She pillowed her head on his shoulder and laid her hand on his chest. "Your heart is pounding."

He let out a chuckle. "You near to killed me, sweetheart."

"Was that a compliment or an insult?" The amusement in her tone told him she knew the answer.

Caleb set his hand over hers and interlaced their fingers. "There's only one thing that could make this day better."

Sara lifted her head to look into his eyes. "Speak for yourself, husband. That was...marvelous." Her eyes brimmed with tears that made his throat tighten. "I never knew what joy could be found between a man and a woman."

"A husband and wife," he corrected.

He wanted her to forget the bastard who'd used her. If Caleb could pluck those memories from her mind, he would. All he could offer, though, was a fresh start and a chance for a real family.

She smiled before laying her head back against his shoulder. "I can think of nothing that could have made *that* better. Of what were you speaking when you said one thing would improve this day?"

Squeezing her against him, he answered her. "If we made a baby, *then* it would be perfect."

Despite talking with Caleb, Sara had been hovering close to sleep, her mind and body exhausted after being up all night to attend Cassie's delivery. The treacherous trips to and from her brother's home, the ordeal of the birth, and Caleb's lovemaking had left her drained. The instant Caleb said the word "baby," she was wide awake. She owed him the truth but could think of no way to explain why she was barren.

He interrupted her thoughts. "You know what?"

"No. What?"

"I've been thinkin' mighty strong 'bout starting a family."

"We've only been married a couple of months," she couldn't help but remind him.

"I know we ain't been together as husband and wife since our wedding night, but once is all it takes sometimes."

"What are you saying, Caleb?"

"I'm sayin' you ain't used the rag bag you made. Not once since we married."

Her face flushed hot. "You shouldn't speak of such things."

"Why? I'm your husband. Your bleeding time is a part of our lives. At least it would be, but you ain't had a bleeding time since we married."

"My monthly should be a private thing," Sara insisted, absolutely mortified to be discussing it with him. "It's none of your concern."

"Didn't mean to embarrass you none," he said, his voice sincere. "But I'm right, ain't I? You ain't used the rag bag because you ain't bled."

She stopped breathing as she mentally counted, clicking off the days, weeks, and then months since she'd arrived in Montana.

Caleb was correct. Her monthly hadn't visited since she'd left Denver. In fact, she'd had only one customer after her last monthly ended.

Drake—the cowboy she'd robbed.

And then Caleb had taken her on their wedding night.

Dear God, what have I done?

No. No, she couldn't have children. Crazy Kate had told her so. The doctor had agreed. Her monthly was simply late. Sara had never had regular cycles, her bleeding often arriving at unexpected time. Perhaps the stress of the last few months had just delayed its arrival.

"You okay?" Caleb's tone was husky with sleep.

She focused on a different issue. "Did you stay up all night?"

"Pert near," he replied. "Needed to check the animals during the storm, then I left mighty early to fetch you."

"I'm so sorry."

"What for?"

"For leaving the chores to you and for making you trek through the storm all the way to Ty's home." At least he wasn't becoming ill from being out in the cold so long.

"Stop it. You were busy helping with the birth." He gave her another squeeze. "Now you'll know what to expect when we have a young'un of our own. I'm sure Cassie and Grace will be with you just like you were with Cassie."

Sara couldn't find the right words to explain why a family was impossible, and her heart warned her it was a mistake to even try. So she only nodded against his shoulder.

"How 'bout we both get some shut-eye? Then we can do afternoon chores together."

She only nodded again.

It wasn't long before soft snores began to slip from Caleb, but Sara could find no rest. Her mind was awhirl with conflicting emotions.

A baby? Had she truly conceived on her wedding night?

She refused to believe God could possibly hate her enough to finally bless her with a caring husband, a home of her own, and— miracle of miracles—a child only to snatch it all away by having Drake sire that child.

If she was having a baby, that infant would be Caleb's and no other's. She convinced herself there was no reason to fret. Drake couldn't have fathered her child. They'd only been together once, and it was directly after her monthly. Surely a woman wasn't fertile so close to her bleeding time.

Ah, but she'd only mated with Caleb once as well, and that had been a mere week after she'd escaped The Palace.

Stop it! You shall drive yourself mad!

Trying to calm her thoughts, Sara closed her eyes and drew in a few deep breaths. Suddenly a new idea popped into her head with startling clarity.

No one from Denver knows I am here.

Even if God proved vengeful and Drake's seed had taken root in her womb, no one would ever have to know. There would never be a person to question her baby's paternity. The child would be hers, and that was all that mattered. The secret—should there be one to reveal—would be forever protected because she would take it to her grave.

A baby?

At that moment, only God knew for sure. Time would tell.

Relief washed over Sara, and she allowed her fatigue to drag her closer to sleep. Her last thought comforted her as much as Caleb's embrace.

The Palace is a part of my past, not my future...

Chapter Fourteen

The drive to town a week later convinced Sara she'd been wrong in thinking she couldn't have a child.

Each bump in the road sent nausea roiling through her, something she tried hard to hide from Caleb. They'd discussed whether she was pregnant on their special night together, but neither had introduced the topic again. Perhaps they were both afraid to hope, although Sara often wondered if their hopes were for the same thing.

She was pregnant. Now there was no doubt. But despite the assurances she'd given herself that the child was surely Caleb's, she harbored frightening concerns that Drake had planted his seed before Caleb had consummated their wedding vows.

When she'd awakened the morning after they'd made love—the day she'd realized she loved her husband—she'd promptly emptied her stomach into the chamber pot. Caleb hadn't been there, so she hadn't needed to come up with an explanation. She'd lied to herself that something she'd eaten had simply caused the upset. That lie didn't hold when the same thing happened the next morning. And the next...

The time had come to face the consequences of her past, no matter how deeply she wanted to bury it. Another bump ended her chance at hiding her secret. She scrambled for the side as her breakfast came back up in a rush.

"Oh, Lord...Sara." Caleb's words were accompanied by the wagon grinding to a halt. "Oh, sweetheart. What can I do to help?"

Sara wiped the back of her mouth with her hand. Thankfully, the weather was unseasonably warm, so she hadn't made a mess all over the scarf that usually covered her face whenever she was outside. "I'm fine now. Must be something I ate," she fibbed.

This wasn't the time or place to explain. When she shared the news, she wanted it to be special. They'd never courted, and their marriage had been rushed. She wanted to make this special, something they could share with their child years from now. Perhaps she should tell him on Christmas Day. She couldn't imagine a better gift.

The wagon lurched into motion with Caleb's letting out a heavy sigh.

He knew. He had to know. But she kept her silence.

The town came into view. Although the scenery on their ride from the farm had been nothing but fields and trees blanketed in white, the city was awash in brown. Mud as far as the eye could see. Since the cold had temporarily eased, people moved about, ducking in different buildings, sharing some conversation on the walkways, trying to balance on the timbers placed in the street to allow crossing over the muddy mess. The townsfolk were bundled in heavy coats, but they seemed at ease with the cold. Perhaps one day, she'd adjust to it as well.

Sara figured their arrival in town was the perfect time to segue into a new topic. "I hope the store has received shipments. With all the snow holding us hostage, our pantry needs restocked."

"That cold spell we just weathered ain't unusual," Caleb replied. "You're gonna have to get used to being stuck in the house for long times."

She nodded. "That's the reason I want to be sure we have a stocked pantry. I don't wish you to go hungry because your wife isn't used to Montana winters. I only hope we're not snowed in for Christmas next week. I would love to see Ty, Cassie, and their daughter. I must see to the welfare of my goddaughter."

"Maybe then we can learn what they named her."

After he stopped the wagon, he climbed down and came around to her side. Hands on her waist, he lifted her to the ground.

Caleb kissed her forehead. "You go on into the store. I need to see about some feed for the animals. I'll be along directly."

"Is there anything special you wish me to purchase?"

"Ain't you got the list?" he asked.

Sara nodded. "I wasn't sure if there was something that you'd forgotten to add."

"I want you to buy yourself something, sweetheart."

"Pardon?"

His smile warmed her from the inside out. "You ain't never asked for nothing. I want you to buy something for you."

"I don't need anything, Caleb."

"You've been wearin' my momma's clothes ever since we got hitched. Buy yourself something pretty you want just for you." He plucked some money from his pocket and pressed it into her gloved palm. "This is for you." He tapped the tip of her nose. "Don't you go spending it on flour or sugar."

"Thank you," she murmured. "You're so thoughtful."

"You're welcome." Caleb strode down the boardwalk, leaving her to her thoughts.

She stood there a long time, watching him walk away. His step held a swagger, a cockiness that she admired and learned to appreciate since he made her feel safe.

How had she found herself so blessed as to have Caleb Young as her husband? She didn't deserve such a wonderful man or such a wonderful life. She hadn't earned it in any way.

But it was hers. *He* was hers.

With a quick prayer thanking her Maker for sending her to him and vowing to be the kind of wife he deserved, she went into the store.

***

Sara let her fingers brush over the soft material. The bolt of fabric had called to her from the moment she saw it. The hue was pink, and small red flowers made a delicate pattern she knew would make a beautiful Sunday dress.

Caleb had told her to spend the money on herself, but she was loathe to follow his orders. He was being far too generous, and those funds could easily be used to help replenish their supplies.

What she truly wanted was a book, one of the few the general store had to offer. The only thing she missed about Denver was that she could so easily find new stories or attend plays. While Caleb might entertain her through the lonely hours of being snowed in on the farm, she longed to sink into a good story.

Since it would be too decadent to spend her husband's funds on a book, she'd shifted to searching through the bolts of cloth. Sewing would give her something to do, and the pink had immediately caught her eye.

"The color would be beautiful on you," a familiar voice said as a hand settled on her shoulder.

"Drew!" Sara whirled to face him only to find herself gathered into his arms for a tight hug.

Finally releasing her, Drew held her by the shoulders and gave her a deliberate sweep from head to toe. "You're looking quite fit, my dear. I feared you would suffer from the harshness of the winters in this territory."

"I'm adjusting. I won't say they're my cup of tea, but…" She shrugged.

He chuckled. "So diplomatic. Had I not grown up near here, I fear I'd have some trouble becoming accustomed to the way the snow piles up. But smile, sweet Sara! Today, the sun is shining, and you're free from our dour Caleb."

"Dour? Caleb isn't dour."

"Oh, my. Are you saying having you as his wife has improved his disposition?" Drew's wink made her face flush hot.

Sara turned back to the material. "He has a fine disposition," she insisted. "Only today he gave me money to buy myself something special. He's generous and kind and—"

Moving to her side, Drew put his hand over hers. "You need not worry so. I was merely teasing. I appreciate Caleb's finer qualities, although I do believe he was growing sullen in his loneliness. You, I'm sure, are a breath of fresh air."

"I assume you have yet to see my husband," she said, feeling the need to tease Drew for his outrageous compliments.

"No. Not today," Drew replied.

"Then how can you judge his mood improved, sir? Perhaps I am a raving shrew he has yet to tame. You might find him quite weary of my company and in a temperament that makes dour appear a mild diagnosis."

Drew's boisterous laugh made heads turn their way.

Unaccustomed to being the center of attention, Sara felt her face heat in embarrassment. She turned her gaze back to the bolt of cloth. "Are you here to restock your pantry as I am?"

"In all honesty," he said, "I was sincerely tired of being confined to the house with Gideon as my only company. I needed to be free for a spell, and Gideon felt the same. So here we are in town. I have read all my books at least five times, and because of the continuous snowstorms in the winter, there are no plays being presented. I yearn for warmer months so I can again find myself on the stage."

"You're an actor?" It dawned on her she knew little about Caleb's brother or his brother's companion.

"I am. Sad to say it's quite difficult to ply my trade in such a small town."

"Then why do you stay? Would you not fare better in California or back East?"

"I would, but I fear Gideon's heart is tied to Montana."

She understood. "And because your heart is tied to Gideon, you go where he goes."

"'For where thou art, there is the world itself, and where thou art not, desolation.'"

Gaping at him, she asked, "Is that Shakespeare?"

Drew nodded. "*Henry the Sixth*. I'm impressed. Are you familiar with Shakespeare's works?"

"Some," she replied. The door was open to share some of her past with Drew, but Sara hesitated. He was clearly well-traveled, and although Denver was worlds away, she worried that something she'd say might trigger a memory. The likelihood their paths had ever crossed was nil. "I would love to borrow some of your books."

"You read?"

Sara nodded. "Caleb only has a Bible. While I enjoy reading the gospels, the rest of the book lacks for…um…"

"Plot?" A deep chuckle rose from his chest. "I shall bring all my books the next time we come to visit. You may read them to your heart's content."

"You'd do that for me?"

"'Come, and take choice of all my library, and so beguile thy sorrow.'"

Since he was wont to quote the Bard, she answered in kind. "'I can no other answer make but thanks, and thanks, and ever thanks.'"

"Very good, Sara! You, Cassie, and I shall have to remember to exchange quotes. She's as adept as you, and I miss her company."

The bell above the store's door rang, and Sara glanced that way, hoping to see Caleb coming for her. Instead, a strange woman hurried inside. She was bundled against the cold, but her brown eyes were wide. She breathed hard, near to panting.

Sara knew that kind of panic and hurried to the woman as the shopkeeper's wife, Mrs. Whyde, did the same. Drew followed close behind.

Taking the woman's gloved hands in hers, Sara smiled, hoping to relieve the fear she saw so clearly. "There is no need to be afraid."

"What's wrong, girl?" Mrs. Whyde asked.

"I...I..." The woman gave her head a shake and withdrew her hands. She seemed to gain a little more control over herself as she removed her gloves and set them on the closest cracker barrel.

Then she untied her knit cap and swept it off her head. Her hair was the color of wheat, and a long braid spilled from the cap down her back. "I'm sorry. I was just frightened for a moment when I exited the stagecoach and found myself alone. I'd hoped someone would meet me when I arrived."

"Ain't likely," Mrs. Whyde said with an inelegant snort. "No one even knew when the next stage would make it across the mountain pass."

"I figured as much, which helped allay my fear." The woman took a deep, steadying breath. "I'm sure if he knew I'd be here today, he would've met me. It was just frightening to be in a new town so far away from home and realize I knew no one here."

Sara smiled. "Well, then, let us remedy that problem by introducing ourselves. I'm Sara Fuller...um...Young. Sara Young." She wasn't sure she'd ever get used to the change in her name.

"Young? That's splendid," the woman exclaimed. "You must be related to the man I'm here to meet. Perhaps you can take me to him, if you'd be so kind."

A painful knot suddenly formed in Sara's stomach, and she had the irrational desire to flee the store as quickly as possible. She swallowed hard, telling herself the fear was unreasonable. Young was a common enough name. Surely this woman had nothing to do with Caleb.

She mentally shook herself when she remembered the last time she'd seen Drew and Gideon they'd been praising the Morgan's housekeeper, Daisy. They'd claimed they were searching for someone to be their housekeeper. This woman had probably come in answer to an ad the men had placed in some newspaper in a larger town.

"Who are you here to see?" Sara asked, expecting to hear Gideon's name.

"I'm here for Caleb Young," the woman replied. Her voice carried a light accent, one that Sara recognized as German.

A wave of nausea had Sara swallowing hard. "Caleb Young? Why are you here for Caleb?"

"I'm his wife."

Chapter Fifteen

Caleb walked into the general store just in time to see Drew catch Sara before she hit the floor.

He rushed to her, jerked off his gloves, and laid his hand on her cheek. "Sara? Sweetheart?" Leveling at glare at Drew, he asked, "What happened?"

Drew glared right back at him. "Don't ask me." He inclined his head toward a petite blonde who looked as confused as Caleb felt. "I'm not the one who committed bigamy. You are."

Since Caleb had no idea what Drew was talking about—which wasn't at all unusual, considering Drew's penchant for dramatic literary quotes—he focused on Sara. Her face was as white as fresh snow. Her fainting and the fact she'd emptied her belly on the ride into town could only mean one thing.

A smile spread from his face to his heart.

Drew let out a low growl. "Sara swoons and you smile? What in the devil is wrong with you?"

"She's carrying," Caleb calmly replied as he stroked his wife's pale cheek.

Drew's scoff came as a surprise. "Well, is that not lovely? Are *both* of your wives expecting your children?"

"What in the hell are you talkin' about?"

With a nod at the blonde, Drew said, "This woman just introduced herself as your wife."

The blonde's eyes flew wide. "You're Caleb Young?"

Caleb nodded, and his mind quickly solved the puzzle Drew had just tossed his way. "Dear Lord. You're here from St. Louis, ain't you? Did Reverend Hayes send you?"

Her lower lip quivered as she nodded. "It would appear I've arrived too late."

With a heavy sigh, he held out his hand. "I'm afraid so. Miss...?"

"Kayla Backer." She shook his hand, her fingers trembling as she pulled them from his grasp.

"She's not truly your wife?" Drew asked, his gaze shifting between Kayla and Caleb.

The man was being outrageous, something he seemed to enjoy. Caleb and Sara had already told Gideon and Drew about the mix-up. "Stop bein' a pain in my ass."

"Ah, but that would ruin my sport!" Drew insisted. After a moment of thought he shook his head. "Poor Miss Backer. It never would have worked, you realize."

"I beg your pardon?" Kayla said, cocking her head.

"You and our Caleb would never have suited," he replied.

"And might I ask why you believe that?"

"Your names." Drew grinned. "Caleb and Kayla are simply too similar. You're clearly meant for another, my dear."

Mrs. Whyde came hurrying from the back room, where she'd scurried after Sara fainted. She slapped the wet cloth she'd retrieved across Sara's forehead. "The poor dear. The shock must've made her faint dead away." She scowled at Caleb. "What kinda game are you playin' with these women, Caleb Young?"

"I ain't playin' a game!" Rolling his eyes, Caleb tried to grab a hold of some patience, but there was none to be found. "Sara and I were married proper."

Mrs. Whyde put her hand on Kayla's arm. "Then why does this poor dear think she's your bride?"

Thankfully, Drew stepped in. Since most of the women in town adored him, flocking to see him acting in the plays put on during the summer and fall, he had a way of charming them and bending them to his will. While he normally found that trait annoying, today Caleb was nothing but grateful.

"My dear Mrs. Whyde," Drew practically purred. "You think so poorly of our Caleb. This is all a simple misunderstanding. When I have some time, I'll stop by for some tea and biscuits and explain the whole, wonderful tale. I dare say we'll share a laugh or two over his predicament."

Mrs. Whyde looked up at him with slumberous eyes, as though she'd fallen under his spell. "That would be lovely."

Kayla was wringing her hands, and Caleb felt as low as a grasshopper's belly. He had no idea what to say to the poor woman, but his main concern was Sara. When she began to stir, Caleb heaved a sigh of relief.

Her hand went to the wet cloth, and she tugged it away. Blinking, she stared into Caleb's eyes. "What...? Where...? Caleb?"

"You fainted, sweetheart." God help him, he couldn't stop smiling. Despite his fears that he would never have a family, the Lord had blessed them with a child.

"I fainted?" A disgruntled frown bowed her lips. "Only weak women faint. You must be mistaken."

"You should take her in back and loosen that corset," Mrs. Whyde insisted.

"No, please." Sara handed her the cloth. "I don't wish to be a bother."

Drew patted her hand. "Are you feeling better, my dear? The shock was simply more than you could bear."

"Shock?" *What shock?*

Sara's head took a long time clearing. Everything was fuzzy, and she couldn't understand what prompted her to faint. Yes, she wore a corset. But since she now dressed herself and had no one to tighten the laces, the corset wasn't uncomfortably tight. Surely not enough to cause a swoon.

"Sara," Caleb said, his voice soft and tender, his eyes full of sparkle. "I think you might be carrying."

"Carrying?" Her realization came flooding back and with her remembrance came a hot flush over her face. While she was pleased to see that her husband was happy about the news, she wanted to share their joy in private. "We shouldn't discuss such things in a public place."

"Especially when your betrothed is listening in," Drew quipped.

The rest of her memories roared back to life. Drew was correct. The shock of Caleb's true bride arriving had caused the swoon.

Sara squirmed in her husband's arms. When he only squeezed her tighter against him, she scolded, "Your bride has arrived. We must see to her welfare."

Caleb let her down easy and sheepishly glanced at the blonde. "*You're* my bride, Sara."

The blonde appeared close to tears. "I shouldn't have come here. I knew it. I just knew it. And then the winter storm delayed me and… I've made a horrible mistake."

Sara's heart went out to the woman. She'd stood in the same shoes months ago, arriving in a strange town with nothing but hopes and dreams. God's grace had put Caleb in her path. But that gift had cost this new woman. This beautiful lady was the one who'd been sent to marry Caleb, and now Sara enjoyed the stability of life with a man she loved.

She'd stolen this woman's life.

The woman was wringing her hands, so Sara went to her and took her hands in hers. "Please don't fret. What is your name?"

"Kayla," the woman replied. "Kayla Backer."

"Well, Kayla Backer… Let me be the first to welcome you to White Pines."

A tear slid down Kayla's face. "But I'm *not* welcome here." Her gaze shifted to Caleb. "I was supposed to be his bride. Reverend Hayes assured me that…" She tugged her hands away and wiped away the tear. "What does it matter now? I have foolishly cast my future to the wind, and now I must find a way back to St. Louis."

"I'll buy you a ticket," Caleb insisted, forcing Sara to glare at him.

Drew cuffed Caleb on the shoulder. "Stop being so inhospitable. You're a lucky man. Most of the single men in the territory would give their right arms to find a wife. You, my friend, have acquired *two*."

"Stop it." Caleb roughly brushed away Drew's hand, a low growl rising from his chest. "Kayla ain't my wife. It's all a misunderstanding."

"Kayla," Sara said. "Such a pretty name. Please do not worry so. You have not cast your future to the wind, as you say. There is much truth in Drew's teasing. White Pines *is* full of men seeking a wife. Good men. God-fearing men. You will have no lack of suitors. Why, I dare say, they shall be lining up to court you."

"Lining up where?" Kayla shook her head. "I have nowhere to stay, no money, and no contacts."

"Well, then..." Without even asking her husband, Sara did what she thought was right—something she hoped would make amends for stealing Kayla's life. "You shall stay on the farm with Caleb and me."

Finally finding the courage to glance at Caleb, Sara breathed a sigh of relief when he gave her a brisk nod.

Proud that she'd held so tightly to her self-control, Sara wanted nothing more than to leave town as quickly as possible, even if that meant dragging Kayla along with them. She was humiliated, afraid the news that she wasn't the bride Caleb had intended would cause the town gossips to turn against her and speculate on how and why she'd come to town.

Her luck had soured, something she'd anticipated. Yet the anger and hurt threatened to drown her. Stomach churning, she tried to remind herself that few people knew how Sara came to be Caleb's wife. Most accepted with only a handful of questions the bare bones story they'd all decided to tell about how Ty had arranged for Sara to meet Caleb. Once they'd met, they'd quickly decided to marry. Conveniently, most of the townsfolk had forgotten Caleb's claim of having a mail order bride coming.

Now that Kayla was here, the truth was sure to come out and their memories would be jogged.

Dear God... Would anyone be able to tie Sara to her past, to the months she'd spent in Denver or the time she'd been Jean-Claude's mistress?

"Sara? Sweetheart?" Caleb tossed her a worried frown. "Don't you go swoonin' on me again."

Mrs. Whyde had taken the wet cloth, but she offered to give it back to Sara. "You've gone pale, child. Put this on your forehead."

"No, thank you. I'm fine. Truly." Sara tried to smile. "Thank you for your kindness." She looked to her husband. "We need to finish purchasing our supplies and get Kayla settled on the farm. Only God knows when the snows will begin again."

Caleb pursed his lips. "You really want her to stay with us? Ain't so sure that's a good idea... I could put her up in the boarding house and—"

Leaning close, Sara dropped her voice to a whisper. "Think of the gossip, Caleb. She should have a place to call home until we can arrange for some introductions to some gentlemen."

His lips remained a grim line. "Ain't so sure that's the proper thing to do."

Drew butt into their whispered conversation. "I believe proper went flying right out of the window when Miss Backer arrived."

Caleb's scowl could have heated the entire town through the long, cold winter.

"Fine." He held out his hand. "Give me the list. I'll get our stuff. You help Miss Backer fetch her trunk and—"

Kayla picked up the carpetbag she'd dropped at her feet. "I have nothing but my satchel."

Caleb was close to shouting his frustration. He was good and mad, but he had no one to direct that anger at except himself.

Drew was right—he'd wanted a wife, and now had two women who needed him.

He snatched the list from Sara's hand and frowned as he watched the women heading to the wagon.

Drew buzzed around him like an annoying mosquito that refused to be swatted. "What I wouldn't give to spend some time in your home right now."

"Go away, Drew."

Picking up a few cans of peaches, he piled them next to the supplies Sara had already assembled on the counter. He scanned the list, realized there was little left to acquire, and breathed a sigh of relief.

"Such excitement!" Drew exclaimed. "Two women vying for your attentions. The other men will be so envious when they hear of your good luck."

"So help me, Drew..."

"And the suitors are sure to start arriving as soon as word spreads that an unattached female is residing in your household. I'd dare to guess that they will line up to meet the beautiful Miss Backer."

Caleb added a few jars of Mrs. Whyde's canned green beans to the stack. "Don't make me break your nose."

"Why would you do that?" Gideon asked as he strode toward them with a grin on his face. "Other than the usual..."

"Oh, my dear Gideon." Drew was practically bouncing in excitement. "I have *so* much to tell you."

His face flushing hot, Caleb dreaded his older brother's reaction to his predicament. While Drew related the story with relish and flourish, Caleb finished finding the supplies and waited as Mrs. Whyde totaled the bill and accepted payment. By the time Drew was done tattling, Caleb had the boxes of supplies loaded in the wagon.

Then he realized what Sara hadn't bought. Something for herself.

"Damn," he mumbled.

"Damn right," Gideon scolded. "What were you thinking, Caleb?"

"This wasn't supposed to happen," he replied. "You know why Sara's here. She's Ty's sister."

"But you're the one who sent for a mail order bride," Gideon countered. "You knew this could happen."

Caleb shook his head. "How could I? Even you thought Reverend Hayes stole my money. Don't tell me you ever expected a woman to show up?"

"You obviously did, and you married the wrong woman because of it." Gideon wiped his hand over his face, sputtering the whole time. "What are you going to do about this, Caleb?"

Drew put his hand on Gideon's shoulder. "There's little to be done about it, Gideon." Thankfully, his tone was serious. "The woman is here, and we all need to make her feel welcome. The poor creature is frightened and alone. We can make sure she finds the right man to marry."

"Marry?" Gideon shot Drew a confused frown.

"Yeah, marry," Caleb replied. "Think about it Gideon… Every man within riding' distance will be wanting to court her."

Gideon rubbed his chin. "Hadn't thought of that… But you're right."

"We shall be sure a man of quality takes her as his wife," Drew said. "Then we will have done our duty by Miss Backer."

Gideon still appeared skeptical. "Think it'll be that easy?"

"Absolutely." Drew gave him a decisive nod. "We'll have her married off in no time. 'Thou art sad: get thee a wife, get thee a wife!'"

Chapter Sixteen

Sara shook out Kayla's dress and laid it on the bed. "We shall have to iron this tomorrow morning. You may share my dresses until we can sew a few new ones for you."

"You needn't bother." Kayla set her brush and looking glass on the small table next to the ceramic pitcher and started unplaiting her braid. "I appreciate your kindness more than you know, but I will be leaving as soon as possible."

"Don't start that again." Guiding Kayla to the bed, Sara pushed her to sit and grabbed the brush. "Let me help." After she'd unbraided Kayla's hair, she brushed the long tresses. "Such a beautiful color."

"Thank you." Kayla's voice was a whisper, and she clenched her hands in her lap until her knuckles blanched.

Despite all Sara had tried to do, she simply couldn't seem to help her guest relax. "The men are right, you know. Once word gets out that there is an unmarried and very handsome woman living on Caleb Young's farm, we shall have to beat them away with a broom."

All Kayla did was shrug.

Sara set the brush aside. "Kayla…you must look on the bright side of things."

Turning to face Sara, Kayla frowned. "I fail to see a bright side. I did something horribly foolish and must now face the consequences." Her lip quivered.

"You're wrong," Sara said with a shake of her head. "It wasn't at all foolish to come to White Pines. Would it ease your worry if I told you I had done the same only a few months ago?"

Another shrug. "I have no idea how you came to be married to the man who paid for *me* to travel here and marry him."

Her accusatory tone stung. Guilt still weighing heavily on her thoughts, Sara tried to explain. "It was circumstances. I would be lying if I told you I wish things were different and that you had met Caleb first. I came here much as you did, with nothing. Had I not married Caleb, I fear my future would have been too bleak to even contemplate."

Kayla's forehead wrinkled and her mouth dropped to a frown. "He knew Reverend Hayes would send a wife. Why would he so impulsively marry you when he'd arranged for another bride?"

"He thought I was you," Sara replied. "I arrived only a short time after the telegram from the reverend, all the way back in September."

"How could he think you were me? For God's sake…we look nothing alike."

"He couldn't have known what you looked like, Kayla. All the good reverend had done was to send a message that a woman would arrive. When I stepped off the stagecoach, he assumed I was that woman. We married rather hastily, before I could straighten out his misassumption, before I even knew there'd been a mistake."

Accusing brown eyes bored through Sara. "But you are obviously an intelligent woman. You had to realize something wasn't right, yet you took vows with the man the same day you met him."

"I know it sounds…contrived." Sara sighed. "I also made an enormous misassumption. I traveled here to meet my brother. The way Caleb greeted me and talked of how I'd been sent to him, I believed my brother had chosen a husband for me. Everything Caleb said seemed to confirm my notion, just as the things I said fit the story that I'd been sent to him. It was all rather serendipitous."

Although her features softened, Kayla still frowned. "I shouldn't be at all surprised by this turn of events. It seems as though the Fates are conspiring against me. Again." She hung her head.

If she hadn't thought her actions would appear condescending, Sara would have patted Kayla on the shoulder and told her to keep a firm resolve, that it would all come out in the wash. "Surely it cannot be *that* bad."

Kayla's head rose until her gaze locked on Sara's. "If you only knew…"

Since the woman didn't expand on that thought, Sara assumed Kayla didn't want to share her story. Her curiosity piqued, she pushed for an answer. "Why did you agree to Caleb's proposition? I would think St. Louis would hold many more prospects than the Montana Territory."

Bounding from the bed, Kayla nervously fidgeted with her brush. "I don't wish to speak of it. I fear I am weary from my odyssey, and I would like to sleep now."

"Odyssey? Didn't you travel here directly from St. Louis?"

An inelegant snort came from Kayla. "This journey has been anything but direct. I left in September."

Sara gasped. "But that was nearly three months ago."

Kayla nodded but didn't explain. "I wish to rest now."

Although Kayla wouldn't say the words, Sara heard them clear as a bell—probably because she'd known girls much like Kayla. She'd *been* a girl much like Kayla. The Palace was full of women escaping things exactly as Kayla had agreed to marry a man she didn't even know.

The very reason Sara had done the same.

I escaped something bad.

Hopefully that "bad" wouldn't follow Kayla to White Pines.

"I shall leave you then." Sara rose and walked to the door before she paused and turned back to Kayla. "Please call should you need anything. Good sleep to you."

She shut the door quietly and padded down the freezing hallway to the bedroom she shared with Caleb, needing to feel his arms around her.

***

Caleb looked up when Sara came into the bedroom. "Did you get Kayla settled?"

Her frown worried him. She nodded and dropped her robe on the foot of the bed.

He held the covers open and waited for her to crawl in beside him. Then he covered his wife and hauled her up against his side. Pressing his lips against her forehead, he murmured, "You're a good woman, Sara Young."

Her derisive snort surprised him.

"You *are*."

"I stole you from Kayla Backer." Her voice quavered with emotion.

Caleb squeezed her tightly. "That ain't the way I see it."

"How else could anyone see it? Kayla came here to be your bride. I was merely your...mistake."

"Did you ever think that you didn't *take* me from Kayla but instead *saved* me from her?"

Sara wiggled higher up his body until her eyes were level with his. "What is that supposed to mean?"

Offering her a smile, he cupped one soft cheek of her backside in his hand, wondering if he'd ever get used to having such a beautiful creature in his bed. "It means I was meant to marry you, not her. God set you in my path to keep me from makin' the biggest mistake of my life."

"But you know nothing about her. Perhaps she'd be better suited—"

Caleb cut her off with a hard kiss. "Don't matter. Ain't nothing that matters. You're the woman I want. I...I... Ah, hell. I love you, Sara."

How had he found the courage to tell her what was in his heart?

He wasn't sure, but he was glad he had. Until he saw her reaction to his declaration. "Dear Lord, that makes you cry?"

She tried to bury her face against his shoulder, but he wouldn't let her.

"Sweetheart, why are you crying? Don't that make you happy?"

"You don't mean it," she wailed.

"Of course I mean it."

When she tried to roll away from him, he held tight. She kept struggling to move until he had no choice but to rise over her and pin her to the mattress with his body. The feel of her beneath him and the pleasant scent of her essence had his cock hardening in desire.

"Sara, stop wiggling and look at me."

Surprisingly, she obeyed. Tears glistened in her eyes.

"Why don't you think I love you?"

She sniffed as the tears spilled over her lashes.

"Don't you dare start cryin' again."

"You can't mean it." A small hiccough escaped. "You only said it because of the baby."

The baby. Kayla's arrival had made Caleb forget about their happy news.

No, when he'd understood he loved Sara, the baby hadn't factored into his realization. Knowing that she carried his child only made him love her more. The problem was in the timing of his revelation. Now he had to convince Sara of his sincerity.

"Ain't you got no faith in me?" he asked.

"Of course I have faith in you." He loved her disgruntled tone.

Caleb cradled her face in his hands, brushing the tears from her cheeks with his thumbs. "Then you're just gonna have to trust me. I ain't saying it 'cause of the baby. The moment I saw Kayla and heard she was the one the reverend sent, I realized what a lucky man I was."

Sara hiccoughed again. "You're speaking in riddles."

"I ain't got the proper words to explain, sweetheart. I ain't like you and Drew, always using fancy words."

Her eyes searched his. "I don't need fancy words, Caleb. Just try to make me understand. Please."

He let out a chuckle and gave her a quick kiss. "I guess when I saw Kayla I saw a right pretty woman and thought that if she'd come before you, I'd have considered myself damn lucky. But, pretty as she was, she weren't the right woman. I'd have missed out on you. That made me know that I love you. Now do you believe me?"

A smile blossomed on her face, and she looped her arms around his neck. "Yes, Caleb. I believe you."

This time, the kiss he gave her wasn't quick. It was deep and thorough and full of all he felt in his heart.

Sara laced her fingers through his hair and deepened the kiss. Her body was on fire for her husband, and his declaration of love still rang in her ears.

When Kayla arrived, Sara had feared for her future and the future of her unborn child. Caleb had stolen away those worries with three simple words.

He tugged at her nightgown, helping her out of it before casting it aside. Then he stripped before settling himself between her thighs. His hard cock lay against her mound, and his hands covered her breasts. "I should've known."

"Known?"

"They're a little bigger." His kissed the valley between her breasts before suckling a nipple.

Sara arched into him, trying not to cry out in appreciation. They had a houseguest, and while it might be rude to make love, she simply couldn't bring herself to ask her husband to stop. She needed him deep inside her, showing her what he felt and letting her lavish his body with her love.

He shifted to her other breast, teasing the nipple with his tongue, swirling around and around, making heat build to a crescendo. Her core throbbed in anticipation, and while she normally loved how slow and positively thorough Caleb was when he loved her, she wanted him inside her. Now.

"I want you, husband," she purred.

"Patience," he said with a light chuckle before disappearing below the covers. He trailed a path down her stomach, stopping to run his tongue around her navel. Then he kissed the curls on her mound.

"Caleb, no."

"Yes," he hissed a moment before he spread her thigh wider. He caressed her folds with his fingers before finally gifting her with the most intimate of kisses.

Sara again threaded her fingers through his hair, holding him against her even if he didn't appear to be in a hurry to leave. The way his tongue stroked her sensitive nub and then stabbed in and out of her sheath had her squirming, the need for release becoming close to unbearable.

"Come to me," she begged. "Now."

"No," he replied, kissing her inner thigh. "Come for me this way, sweetheart." His tongue delved into her again.

Unable to fight her release, she bit hard on her bottom lip to keep from screaming her delight. Surge after surge of heat shot through her as Caleb wrung every last tremor from her body. Only when she panted for breath did he kiss his way back up her body.

He knelt between her thighs, his cock at her threshold. "I love you, Sara." He thrust deep inside her as he said the words.

Her greedy body flared back to life, and she wrapped her legs around his hips, trying to pull him as deeply inside her as she could.

Easing back, he waited a quick second before plunging in again. "God, you feel good."

"So do you."

They were the last words she could speak as he forced her higher and higher, building the tension inside her with each thrust until she thought she'd go mad. Biting his shoulder, she let him know she needed him to plunge faster and deeper.

Caleb obliged her, meeting the rhythm of her rising hips until he panted for breath and she held hers.

The second climax made lights flash behind her closed eyelids, and this time, she cried out his name as she reached the splendor only her husband could give her.

A few fast thrusts, and he joined her, spilling his hot seed deep inside her as he breathed her name in her ear.

"God almighty," he said as he tucked his face against her neck. His hot breaths brushed over her skin, raising gooseflesh. "You're gonna kill me one of these days, wife."

"Thank you, husband."

Propping himself up on his elbows, he stared into her eyes. "You ain't said it yet."

Sara knew what he needed to hear but simply couldn't resist the urge to tease. "Said what?"

His growl was rather impressive. "Sara…"

"I love you, Caleb Young. With my whole heart."

Chapter Seventeen

The first suitor arrived only a few minutes past dawn.

Caleb was sipping a cup of coffee when the knock sounded. He'd slept later than usual, feeling a bit tired and more than a little smug. He'd awakened Sara in the wee hours to make love to her again, needing to hear her declarations of love. Nothing had ever sounded as sweet as his wife telling him she loved him while he was deep inside her tight heat.

He'd let her sleep as well, not bothering to wake her when he rose. She'd murmured her displeasure when he'd lifted the covers to get out of bed, but once he tucked the quilts around her, she'd smiled and drifted back into deep sleep. She'd earned the right to catch another hour of rest, and he was quite capable of making his own coffee.

Kayla hadn't stirred yet, so Caleb didn't disturb her. He had no idea what to say to the woman and wanted nothing more than to get her out of his house. While he should've felt guilty for the predicament he'd forced on her, he knew Drew was right. Kayla would have no trouble finding another man to marry. And Caleb meant every word he'd said to his wife. Sara had saved him from his dreary existence. No other woman could ever mean as much to him, and knowing she carried his child made contentment settle on his soul.

The knocking continued, so Caleb strode to the door and jerked it open, ready to tear into whoever was daring to disturb his peace and quiet.

Dale Jacobs stood on the porch, hat in hand. The normally scruffy farmer had shaved, slicked back his hair, and donned in his Sunday best. He smelled of toilet water, something far too flowery for a burly man like Dale. "I, um, I…heard in town 'bout a new lady stayin' at your place. Heard she weren't married or nothin'. I'd be right grateful if you'd introduce me to her."

Caleb couldn't stop a laugh when two more men rode up the road to his house as Dale scowled at them.

No, Kayla would have no trouble finding a husband. He also had no doubt his door would be opening the rest of the day to admit her suitors. He, however had a huge problem. How could he prevent fights among the men vying for one of the few single women to ever come to White Pines?

Since he'd made it his responsibility to make sure she ended up with a good man, Caleb leveled a hard stare at Dale. "Ain't surprised to see you here. I imagine the gossip's flying around town."

"Sure is," Dale said with a nod. "That's why I got here first. Want to snatch her up a'fore any other bastard does."

"She ain't gonna be *snatched up*, Dale. Sara and I want to be sure she marries proper."

"Oh, I'm gonna marry her. Wouldn't disgrace her by draggin' her to my cabin a'fore I take her to the preacher." His hands kept working around the brim of his hat, nervously turning it in a circle. "I was here first, Caleb Young. You best let me in or—" Dale's eyes grew as wide as saucers. "Sweet Jesus." He let out a low whistle.

Caleb glanced back to find Kayla standing in the room, dressed in her robe. He had to admit she made a pretty picture. Slender yet rounded in all the right places. She'd let her hair down, and the wavy mass swirled around her shoulders.

Looks like hers? She could marry any man she wanted.

Dale tried to push his way into the house.

Caleb blocked Dale's path and shoved him back with a hard shoulder against his chest. The two other men had dismounted and were racing across the yard toward the house.

He barked at Kayla over his shoulder. "Go wake Sara and get dressed. I'll deal with these rattlesnakes."

With a quick nod, she hurried down the hall.

The three men stood clustered in the doorway. On tiptoes, they craned their necks to try to get a glimpse of Kayla. Damn if three more riders weren't heading toward the farm, and Caleb spotted a wagon in the distance.

"Ain't none of you coming in," he said, his voice stern.

All of the men loudly protested that statement.

Caleb just shook his head. "I ain't setting you pack of hungry wolves on that poor woman's trail. And I sure as shit ain't letting you trample mud all over Sara's clean floor."

"We got a right to see her!" one of them shouted.

"I was here first!" Dale countered. "Damn your hide, Caleb Young. I had first claim. You know I did."

"She ain't a piece of land, Dale. Let Sara and me bring her into town later. We'll talk to the reverend and see what he thinks is best."

The grumbling grew louder.

"I ain't changing my mind. You all go on home. Kayla's my responsibility, and I'm gonna do right by her."

"Heard she was s'posed to marry *you*," John Tucker said. "Heard you ordered yourself two brides and now you're fixin' to keep 'em both."

"That's foolish talk," Caleb replied. While he could have explained, he saw no reason to give any credence to the rumor, even if it was partly true. "Sara's my wife. Kayla ain't gonna change that."

The other riders had reined their horses to skidding halts.

Caleb raised his voice so they could hear as well. "Now, you all best listen to me and heed my words. Kayla Backer ain't coming out to see none of you. Any of you start sniffing 'round here, I'll make damn sure you *never* get to meet her."

Dale narrowed his eyes. "I ain't givin' up that easy. No sir. Ain't going away without my bride."

"She ain't your bride, and no one said you had to give up," Caleb insisted. "Just want you all off my farm. You want to meet her?" They all nodded, even the two who'd joined them on the now far-too-small porch. "Then you best stop everyone between here and town and tell 'em we'll bring Miss Backer to town this afternoon. We'll take her to church, talk to the reverend, then we can make introductions."

God, he felt like a heel. She'd have her choice of a husband, but she wouldn't even know the man she picked. He didn't see any other way to handle her problem, though. These men wouldn't stop pursuing her, and she couldn't keep staying with him and Sara. That wouldn't be fair to his wife, to have a constant reminder that Caleb should've married another woman.

All the men started protesting, but Caleb just shook his head. "Told you already, I ain't changing my mind. So you best get moving. Any more rascals come knocking on my door, we'll make you all wait one more day for each person who disturbs us. Got it?"

After a lot of griping and whining, they finally gave him their acceptance by nodding and trudging off the porch as though their legs were made of lead.

"Good. Now git! Go on with the lot of you!" He slammed the door, grumbling to himself all the way to the kitchen.

Sara was awake, no doubt from the racket. She was pouring some of the coffee he'd made into two cups. Damn good thing he'd made a huge pot. The day would require a lot of good, strong coffee to brace all of them.

"Who was that man?" Kayla asked.

Caleb figured the best way to handle the issue was head on. "That there was Dale Jacobs. He works some land north of town. He came to marry you."

A gasp slipped from her lips. "But he doesn't even know me. How did he even discover I was here?"

"They," he calmly corrected.

"I beg your pardon?"

"How many were there, Caleb?" Sara asked.

As astute as she was, it didn't surprise him she'd quickly understood. "Five, and more on the way."

Kayla stared at him wide-eyed. "You mean to say there were more men, all here for me?"

Sara nodded. "You're a single woman—a very pretty single woman—in a territory full of lonely men."

"But–but surely they weren't all here simply to see me." Kayla's disgruntled frown almost made Caleb laugh.

She really had no idea about the men in the Montana Territory. While there were families, most of the people making their lives here were men. Single men. Had she arrived only this morning, there would've already been men waiting for a chance to court her.

He sat down at the table next to his wife, again realizing what a lucky man he was to have been the one who met Sara the day she'd arrived. He'd been even luckier that their misunderstanding of each other didn't prevent them from taking vows right away. He could've lost her to one of the many men who would've wanted her, some men who had more money or more land. Certainly some were more attractive.

But she was his. They could scrap like tomcats over Kayla Backer all they wanted. Sara was spoken for.

He took her hand in his, wanting to drag her back to the bedroom and make love to her again. Finding the courage to open his heart had made their bond stronger, and he would've been content to stay in bed with his beautiful wife for the next week, doing nothing but making love to her, watching her sew or read, and holding her close at night.

A good blizzard might do the trick.

The world wouldn't allow them his version of a honeymoon. Not until the matter of Kayla Backer was solved.

"What are we going to do about the men?" Sara squeezed his hand before drawing hers away to cradle her ceramic mug and sip her coffee.

"They ain't comin' back."

"How do you know that?" Kayla still looked as nervous as a cat in a room full of rocking chairs.

"Sent 'em back to town and told 'em to make damned...er...darned sure that every other man they passed knew to stay away from my farm. Told 'em we'll take you into town this afternoon to see Reverend David. He can help us sort this out."

Sara shivered once before she reached for Caleb's hand again. Hearing how the men were clamoring for a chance to win Kayla's hand reminded her far too much of the hassle men made at The Palace on paydays. Every cowboy and his brother fussed and sometimes fought for the prettiest whore or the one who was their favorite amongst the working girls.

Caleb had saved her from that—from her life of shame and humiliation.

Her heart went out to Kayla, and Sara wished there was another solution to the dilemma. Before she could give voice to her concerns about expecting Kayla to choose a husband from the anxious men of White Pines, a knock sounded.

"Damn it all to Hell." Caleb shoved his chair back and stood. "Gonna knock some people into the mud if they don't listen to what I'm telling 'em."

Sara would have followed if she'd been dressed. Since she and Kayla were in their robes, she didn't think it was a good idea for them to be greeting company.

"I hate this." Kayla stared at her cup. "This isn't what I wanted. Not in the least."

"What *did* you want?" Sara asked. She didn't want to pry, but if they were going to find the best solution to Kayla's situation, they needed more information. While Kayla obviously came here to accept Caleb's offer, something had sent her running. Sara felt it in her bones.

Now they needed to know what.

Kayla shrugged and fiddled with the mug. "Does it even matter? Nothing is turning out at all as I expected."

"Do you wish to stay? Or do you wish to return to St. Louis?"

"There's nothing for me there."

"Nothing at all? No family? No friends?"

"Nothing." Kayla dropped her chin, letting her hair partially curtain her face. "I don't wish to talk of St. Louis any longer. I cannot believe I have made such a mess of my life." She closed her eyes and took a deep breath.

Although Sara hadn't learned the specifics, she knew one important thing. Kayla was a strong woman who had endured a great deal. Everything about her spoke of being a survivor. She deserved a peaceful future, the same type of future Sara had found in White Pines.

"We'll make this work, Kayla. I promise you that. You came here looking for a new start, am I right?"

Kayla gave her a brusque nod.

"Then remember one important thing—'A happy ending cannot come in the middle of a story.'"

"Or so says William Shakespeare." Drew smiled from where he leaned his shoulder against the entryway to the kitchen.

"Drew!" Sara glanced down at her robe. "Although I am pleased to see you, Kayla and I aren't dressed properly to receive guests."

"I'm not a guest, my dear. I'm family." His gaze shifted to Kayla, who pulled her robe so tightly closed it covered her neck.

Sara would have to explain about Gideon and Drew's relationship to help put Kayla's mind at ease. They were not amongst the men clamoring to marry her.

"How are you faring, Miss Backer?" he asked.

Instead of replying, Kayla merely shrugged again.

Knowing Kayla was close to losing the emotional self-control she clearly prized, Sara tried to ease her mind. "I was just explaining to Kayla that we will all work together to solve her situation. We shall be sure her life here is everything she expected, and we shall help her find a husband."

"Ah, but I have a *better* solution to propose than marriage," Drew said, coming into the kitchen and giving Kayla a small bow. "Gideon and I would like to invite you to come live with us."

Chapter Eighteen

Once Drew extended the invitation, Sara was sure she'd caught his train of thought. "You wish for Kayla to become your housekeeper?"

Drew nodded as Gideon and Caleb joined them in the kitchen.

After striding over to Sara, Drew picked up her hand and brushed a kiss over her knuckles. "As astute as ever, my dear." Then he turned to Kayla. "Gideon and I are in need of someone to run our household. After meeting you, we could think of no one we would rather have in our home."

Kayla's gaze kept darting around the room as though she were lost and confused.

Sara tried to ease her guest's mind. "Think about it, Kayla. Should you go to live with Gideon and Drew, you will not have to marry so quickly. You'll have time to meet different men and get to know them better."

"Marry in haste, repent in leisure," Gideon added. "Or so I've heard..."

"I know nothing of caring for a household," Kayla said. "Wouldn't there be gossip should I live with two unmarried men?"

"About that..." Drew looked to Gideon, who gave him a curt nod. "Gideon and I are not men who are seeking wives. Nor, I dare say, would anyone in White Pines pass tales about you being...*involved* with either of us."

"Why wouldn't you want—" Kayla's eyes widened. "Are you saying...?"

With a sigh, Drew nodded. "Must I say the words?"

Kayla gave him a vigorous shake of her head. "Oh dear. I have never...er... Oh dear."

"Precisely," Drew said. His features were pinched, and he was clearly uncomfortable with the topic.

Sara thought it unique that so many in the town still kept company with Drew and Gideon. Perhaps the townsfolk either didn't know that the men were in love with each other, or perhaps they simply chose to ignore that fact. Both were treated with the same affection and familiarity as any other White Pines citizen, an anomaly in her limited experience. Tolerant people were few and far between.

Jean-Claude had once been offered a business venture with a man who was suspected of favoring men rather than women. When that suspicion was confirmed, Jean-Claude ended their association in a very public manner, calling the man an "abomination against God." Sara had thought that man was kind, nothing more. She shuddered as she remembered he'd committed suicide not long after Jean-Claude's public shaming. When she'd heard the horrid news, she'd vowed to never judge a person in such an unforgiving and intolerant manner, something Jean-Claude had seemed to enjoy.

She shook her head to try to dislodge the unpleasant memories and focused on the problem at hand. "Drew and Gideon are...discreet. The town accepts them. They are also kind and will pay you a fair salary."

"What would you need me to do for you?" Kayla asked.

"Cook," Drew replied. "Clean. Keep our clothes washed. Perhaps assist us with our gardening. All the things that men seem less than capable of performing adequately."

"We'd give you room, board, and, as Sara said, a salary," Gideon added.

Sara thought their proposition was a wonderful solution, not only for Kayla but for herself. If Kayla was set up as a housekeeper, perhaps the townsfolk wouldn't feel the need to swap stories about unintended brides.

"Think of it, Kayla. They live only a short distance from here. You and I could visit often." The words were out before she realized how much Kayla must dislike her. While Sara and Caleb had taken her in, Kayla wouldn't have needed a home if Sara hadn't stolen Caleb. "Of course you wouldn't have to come here again. Should you wish, you would never have to see me again unless our paths crossed in town."

Kayla's brow furrowed. "But why wouldn't I want to see you? You've shown me so much kindness."

With a shrug, Sara chose not to reply.

"I ain't saying the men who came here this morning ain't nice guys," Caleb said. "But I think you really oughta get to know a man better before you let him drag you to the altar."

"Ain't you one for giving advice you don't take to heart," Gideon said with an elbow in Caleb's ribs.

"'Without counsel plans fail,'" Drew said.

"'But with many advisors, they succeed,'" Kayla retorted with a lopsided smile.

Drew clapped his hands as a smile lit his face. "A woman who can quote the Bible! That seals the deal. You *must* come and be with us, Miss Backer. I need someone who understands my love of quotes. The Bard. The Bible. Philosophers. Only Cassie Bishop and our darling Sara play that game with me, but now I shall have you close at hand. Tell me, my dear...do you enjoy the works of William Shakespeare?"

She nodded. "I wish I'd had the opportunity to read more, but I have only had the pleasure of reading *Romeo and Juliet* and *Hamlet*."

"Then come to our home," Drew insisted. "You may use our

library—"

"*His* library," Gideon added.

"—at your leisure."

"You have books?" Kayla was practically bouncing on her chair.

"I do," Drew replied. "And when your duties are completed, you may read to your heart's content."

"We got a room on the other side of the kitchen," Gideon said. "It could be yours if you wanted. Drew and me...um...we sleep upstairs."

"Got a bed stored in the barn," Caleb offered. "Cassie used it when she stayed here. Ain't got no use for it now."

"Cassie?" Sara tried to bite back the jealousy that threatened to close her throat. She sounded as though she'd swallowed a frog. "Cassie lived *here*?"

"For a while. A short while." Caleb rubbed the back of his neck. "She was new in town. Didn't have nowhere else to go."

"Are you in the habit of taking in women, Mr. Young?" Kayla asked, her voice as strained as Sara's. "First you live with this Cassie, then you marry Sara, both while knowing you'd sent for me? Perhaps it is for the best that you were already married when I arrived. I cannot abide by a man who cannot hold to his vows."

Sara was still struggling with her jealousy. She'd never felt the like before. Envy, perhaps, when she saw another young woman with a fancy new dress or a particularly fashionable hat—things she could never afford.

But this jealousy made her miserable. Her stomach had dropped to her feet, her heartbeat pounded in her ears, and images of slapping Cassie across her pretty little face hit her from every angle. "You were betrothed to Cassie?" She whispered the question to keep herself from shouting her hurt and fury.

"Not betrothed," Caleb said, his eyes settling on anything but her face. "Not...really."

"She refused his proposal," Gideon said.

"She lived here with you but refused to marry you?" Sara's anger grew as she realized the insult they'd dealt Ty. Cassie was his wife. Had her brother taken Cassie as his bride to save her tattered reputation?

From what Sara had seen, Ty loved his wife. But he'd never shared the story of how he came to be married to her.

Nausea washed over Sara, and she swallowed hard to force the bile back down her throat.

Caleb came to her, settling his hands on her shoulders. "Listen to me, Sara. Please?"

She raised her eyes to lock with his.

"I never *lived* with Cassie. She and Drew stayed in a cabin on the farm when they first got to town. That's all. I asked her to marry me, but she wanted your brother."

Although she was still confused, Sara felt her anger ease. Caleb's sincerity was crystal clear, and just knowing he hadn't shared a home with Cassie stole away the jealousy.

Love was tricky business and was turning out to be so different than she'd ever expected. Instead of the sunshine, roses, and poems she'd always believed represented love, she'd found worry, fear, and jealousy. Only when she was alone with Caleb, when he could speak freely of his feelings, did she enjoy the emotion and know what inspired the songwriters and poets. The rest of the time, love made her downright miserable.

Oh, yes, love was tricky business.

"You trust me, don't you, Sara?" Caleb asked.

"I do."

"Then trust me when I say I ain't never felt about Cassie the way I feel about you."

Her husband's vow stole away the last of her jealousy. She gave him a nod and a wan smile.

"So..." Drew pulled Kayla to her feet. "Will you take us up on our offer?"

"Yes," Kayla replied. "I do believe I will."

***

"How did it go in town?" Sara asked as she helped Caleb out of his winter gear. "Where there a lot of men there to meet Kayla?"

"'Bout twenty," he replied. "All of 'em were good and riled up. Had to break up a couple of fistfights. Reverend David got 'em settled down pretty quickly, though."

Judging from the amount of snow clinging to him, winter had returned with a vengeance. She didn't mind if they were soon snowed in. Their pantry was stocked, there was plenty of firewood and lamp oil, and she finally had her husband to herself again.

The drama had drawn to a conclusion.

Kayla's arrival had frightened Sara more than she chose to share with anyone, especially in light of the woman's beauty and grace. But Caleb's intended bride was now with Drew and Gideon, and Sara had Caleb all to herself.

"Heavens. So they didn't take the news well?" she asked as she draped his wet scarf and hat over the chair to dry.

Caleb snorted as he hung his coat next to hers. "Not very good at all. Dale Jacobs is still mighty angry he ain't got her to himself."

"You got her settled in with your brother and Drew?"

He nodded. "She's outta our hair now, sweetheart." After he shed the second heavy shirt he'd donned against the cold, he came to tug her into his embrace. "I'm so sorry about all this nonsense."

"Why would you feel the need to apologize?"

"I'm the one who brought her here and dumped her in your lap." He brushed a kiss over her forehead. "I'm sorry for that."

"You couldn't have known she'd arrive, Caleb. For all you knew, Reverend Hayes wasn't a man of his word. So much time had passed since his message, you had to assume she was never coming."

"I s'pose... Thank you for being so understandin' about all of it."

"Thank *you* for being so understanding. I'm very lucky to have you, Caleb Young."

Caleb's lips touched hers—a swift, short kiss that left her wanting more.

A shiver raced the length of his body. "I'm freezing. Let's go to bed and share some body heat." As he stared down into her eyes, he gave his eyebrows a suggestive waggle. "Can think of lots of ways to generate some warmth. All of 'em require you and me to be naked."

Her love for him swept over her, making Sara breathe a contented sigh. Their problems were behind them now. The rest of the winter they could learn more about each other and wait for their child to be born. Life had taken a turn for the better, and she wasn't a foolish woman. She wouldn't dare risk this wonderful new life by sharing any of her worries with Caleb.

But she still harbored a few... All of them surrounding her time at The Palace.

Her past would stay firmly in her past. Caleb need never know she'd worked for Crazy Kate. The child Sara carried would be her husband's by law if not by blood. Even if another man had planted the seed, this baby would only know Caleb as its father.

With a hard swallow, she tried to bury all the difficult memories deep inside her, wanting never to face them again.

Caleb lifted her chin with a crooked finger. "Sara? Sweetheart? What's wrong?"

Pushing the last of her worries aside, she offered him a smile. "For the first time in my life, nothing. Absolutely nothing."

Chapter Nineteen

Spring was always Sara's favorite time of year. The flowers would force their way through the cold ground, and shoots of green would remind her that the world was in a period of renewal. Rebirth.

A shame the Montana Territory didn't understand that the winter season was supposed to change...

Sweeping last night's dusting of snow off her porch steps, Sara stopped to arch her back and relieve the light cramp that had formed. Nearly eight month's gone, she grew a little more uncomfortable every day. Seemed that all of her weight had shifted low on her hips, and she walked back on her heels like a duck. Caleb even teased her by making quacking sounds whenever she lumbered across the bedroom in the middle of the night to relieve her bladder yet again.

A glance around revealed not a single hope-inspiring spot of green rising from the blanket of snow. April was nearly over and still the snows came. Would the chill never end? As her pregnancy progressed, Sara's tolerance of the cold plummeted. She draped a shawl around her shoulders constantly, even when the fire burned high, and she'd started wearing two pairs of socks to bed every night. Even Caleb's warmth couldn't banish the cold.

Oh, how she wished spring would find its way to Montana.

She glanced up at the sounds of hoof beats, shielding her eyes from the bright morning sunshine that brought little heat with its brilliant rays. Ty was riding a Bay up the long road to her home. She finished sweeping away the snow, propped the broom against a post, and waited for Ty to dismount.

One look at his face told her something was wrong. While Ty wasn't much for smiling, the scowl he wore today was worse than his usual cynical expression.

"What's happened?" she asked before he'd finished tying up his horse. "Is Cassie ill? Is Diana ill?"

"Cassie and the baby ain't sick." The anger she'd seen in his eyes was now fixed firmly on her. "Just heard there's a new man in town."

"I fail to see how a new resident of White Pines has you so distressed."

"He's asking about *you*."

"Me? Who on earth—?" Sara's heart leapt, slamming against her ribcage so hard she could barely breathe.

"Don't know," Ty replied. "Ain't seen him yet. I'm ridin' to town to find out but figured you'd want some warning. The bastard rode into town yesterday. Adam Morgan talked to him. Told me about him this morning because Adam thought he was so peculiar. The man was askin' all around about a woman. He ain't using your name, but—"

"Then how do you know he's searching for me?"

"He's looking for a dark-haired woman who came from Denver last autumn named Princess."

Princess. The name Crazy Kate had chosen for Sara to use with the customers. It had been an insult heaped on her the day Jean-Claude had sold her to the madam. Kate wanted Sara to realize how far she'd fallen in the world so she could keep Sara under her boot heel.

Sara's mind whirled and twirled so fast she suddenly found herself lightheaded. Gasping for breath, she leaned heavily against the post, knocking down the broom.

"Sara?" Ty grabbed her arm. "You gonna swoon?"

"I–I don't know." She slowly bent her knees until she could sit on the porch step. "No...I...I..."

Closing her eyes, she took a deep breath to try to regain some control. The baby was kicking hard, as though he could feel her panic. She rested her hand on her burgeoning belly, trying to soothe her child. And herself.

Her world had come crashing down around her. The past had somehow managed to resurrect from the grave where she'd assumed it would stay buried. Now, it was lumbering at her like one of the undead she'd heard about when a girl from New Orleans, a Creole, worked at The Palace. The stories had frightened Sara to the point of nightmares.

Seemed her nightmares were now coming true. There weren't people rising from their tombs. No, her past was the zombie that would relentlessly search her out and threaten the life she now lived. Should Caleb discover her secret, that life would be coming to an end.

Dear God, what will I do?

"Sara?" Ty crouched down to bring his eyes level to hers. "What are we gonna do to fix this?"

"We?"

His anger visibly grew. "Of course *we*. You're my sister, ain't you?"

She nodded even though she knew there was nothing Ty could do to help her.

"We'll fix this," he said, his tone worthy of a vow.

She nodded again despite her fears and then tried to stand. Her bulk made the task difficult, but he helped her to her feet with a gentle hand on her elbow.

"If I can find Caleb, I'll bring him back with me. We can talk to him about what the man wants from you."

"No! Caleb can't know!"

"Think, Sara. Ain't it better coming from you than hearin' about your past from gossips?"

Although Ty was right, she couldn't imagine confessing to her husband. She'd lose him. For good.

Why had this man come? Why now, when her life was magical and perfect?

Who was he anyway?

A face flashed in her mind, and she suddenly knew exactly who'd come to White Pines.

Drake. The man she'd robbed.

Oh, yes... Her theft of his payroll had prompted him to hunt her down. Not that she blamed him. It had been a healthy sum. But the patience and persistence it must have taken to find her were staggering to the imagination.

"Do you know his name?" Sara asked.

Ty shook his head. "Adam didn't say." Heading back to his horse, he threw himself into the saddle before glaring down at her. "Don't you go thinkin' about going into town on your own. I'll go for Caleb first, then I'll hunt that other rascal down."

"The stranger's name is Drake. I'm sure it's Drake."

"How do you know that?"

"He has a good reason to come for me. I–I..." Tears blurred her vision. "I stole his payroll, Ty. That's how I paid my way to get here."

"How could he find you?"

"I don't know... Crazy Kate? She always told me the walls had eyes and ears. Perhaps she told him my plans."

"You must'a stolen a lot to make him come all this way."

"He had the payroll for his whole staff."

Ty let out a low whistle. "Where's it now?"

"Spent some of it on the train and stage coach. I buried the rest in my flowerbed."

"Well, dig it up. We'll offer him what you've got left and find a way to pay the rest."

"You've got to get to Drake first. He can't talk to Caleb."

Thankfully, she saw no condemnation in her brother's eyes. "I'll find him...and I'll shut his damn mouth. I promise, Sara. I'll protect you. But you've gotta come clean with Caleb. It's the only way to make things better. Don't let him hear it from that Drake feller."

She dropped her gaze to where her hand rested on her belly. If she let Ty see her eyes, she worried he would realize any promise she made to stay put would be a lie. She had to dig up that money and find Drake first, to talk to him, to show him there was more at stake than money.

How could she possibly pay him back? It wasn't as if she could go to her husband and tell him she was not only a whore but a thief and that she needed money to pay off her last customer for stealing from him?

No matter what Ty said, she couldn't tell Caleb. She just couldn't.

"I'll be back before sundown," Ty said. "Where's Caleb anyway?"

"He's at Gideon's. Their mare was having a difficult time foaling. He went to help. He was going to go into town after to... Oh, God. Drake will tell him! He'll find Caleb and tell him!"

"I'll ride for Gideon's to try and find Caleb first." Without a farewell, Ty reined his horse around and headed back down the road.

Sara watched him leave, shivering in fear and dread.

She wanted to be sure Ty was gone for good before she did what she knew needed to be done. Time passed in agonizing slowness until his image had disappeared. Only then did she move.

She was going to dig up the money from the flowerbed and find Drake first. It was the only solution. She would find him and promise to pay him back. Somehow. He'd agree. He just had to. There was too much at stake for him to refuse. She'd find a way to make him understand.

First, she ran to the barn. She was so upset it took it forever to find the spade. When she did, she went straight to the flowerbed that was currently nothing but a snow-covered patch of bare ground.

Cassie was going to help Sara plant marigolds when it turned warmer. And then tulip and crocus bulbs in the fall. Seemed karmic that the little area was nothing but barren—the same thing her heart would be should she lose Caleb.

The dirt was frozen. She found that out when she tried to stab the spade into the dirt. The metal barely scratched the snowy surface. Again and again she tried to force the spade to move the earth. Each time it refused.

Sara tried one last time. Lifting the spade high in front of her, she slammed it into the dirt with both hands. At least this time it pierced the surface, but this would be a long, difficult process at best. There had to be a better way.

She let out a frustrated cry, clenching her hands into fists and wanting to hit something. How was she supposed to fight the frozen flowerbed when it refused to yield?

Whirling on her heel, she hoped Caleb had a pickax in the barn. Three running steps away, she slid on a patch of ice and went down. Hard.

Flat on her back, Sara gasped for breath. She'd struck her head on one of the mountain stones she and Caleb had used to line the path to the barn. Pain crashed over her entire body in waves that seemed unrelenting, and the world swum in a vortex of twisting colors and cold winds.

Lifting a shaking hand, she felt for the injured spot on her head but stopped when another sensation appeared. Something hot and wet rushed between her thighs.

Her water had broken.

No.

No, no, no.

When she tried to push up on her elbow, the first contraction hit, making her curl to her right side and pant with the pain. Her head throbbed, as did her back, while her womb squeezed tight enough to make her cry out. Blackness threatened to claim her, but Sara fought against it. She had to get help. Now.

The labor pain eased, and her thoughts became fragmented and scattered like snowflakes in the winter breeze. She fought hard to stay awake, but she was rapidly losing the battle.

Sara's last thought before darkness claimed her was crystal clear.

Dear God, please save our baby.

***

Caleb hefted the last sack of grain into the back of his wagon before a yawn shook his whole body. Once he got home, he'd grab Sara and head straight to bed. Being as she napped often now, he could coax her to snuggle up against him while he finally caught some shut-eye. He slept better when he could hold her close.

The foal had been a difficult delivery, but with his help, the little brown colt and his mama had survived. A satisfying outcome, even if it had cost Caleb a night's rest. An easy price to pay.

"Caleb!" Ty's shout came from down the road.

"Over here!" Waving his arms, he tried to get Ty's attention.

Ty waved back, and before too long, he was throwing himself from the saddle and marching at Caleb with a hot scowl plastered on his face.

"Is there a problem?" Caleb asked when Ty reached his side.

Instead of replying, Ty gave him a good head-to-toe appraisal, as though searching for something amiss. Then his tension eased. "We need to get back home."

Panic hit like a blow to the midsection. "Is Sara in trouble?"

"You could say that."

"Speak plain, man! Is it the baby?"

"Sara's healthy, if that's what you're talkin' about. She needs you, though."

Ty had always seemed a bit stiff and reserved, but now he was acting downright agitated. Although Caleb had no idea what had Ty so restless, he would oblige him since his errands were done. "I'm fixing to head home right now. Okay?"

"I'll follow you." Ty grabbed his horse's reins.

"Why?"

"Told you," Ty said, climbing onto his saddle. "Sara needs you."

"What in the devil's gotten into you?"

"Hurry, Caleb." Then a word slipped from Ty's lips that Caleb had never heard the man utter before. "Please."

A cold chill ran the length of Caleb's spine, and he rapidly untied his horses and got into the wagon.

Hurry, Caleb. Please.

This time the words filling his mind were spoken in Sara's sweet voice.

"Follow me," Caleb called to Ty before slapping the reins against the horses' rumps. "We'll get there right quick."

***

"Princess?" A cold hand stroked Sara's forehead. "Wake up, Princess."

The voice was familiar, calling from a distance. Sara struggled to open her eyes.

The moment light seeped through her eyelids, pain sliced through her head. She groaned and threw an arm over her face only a moment before her womb painfully contracted.

Everything came rushing back as the agony gripped her. With the labor pain came a rush of more hot wetness between her thighs. All she could do was pant through the contraction and try to keep the blackness from encroaching again. As the pain peaked and then eased, she raised a trembling hand to the sore spot on the back of her head.

A hand seized her wrist. "Don't. It's bleeding. We need to clean and maybe stitch the wound."

Sara finally opened her eyes to the haunting voice.

Drake. Drake had found her.

"What happened?" he asked.

"I fell. The baby... Oh, God. The baby!"

When she struggled to rise, Drake gripped her shoulders. "Don't move. You're bleedin'."

"So you said."

"No, darlin'. Not your head. The baby..."

The sticky moisture wasn't just her water. The baby was in danger. "Please God, no."

"I need to get you inside." He stood and then scooped her into his arms as though she weighed nothing. With surprising ease, he went up the porch stairs and opened the door. "Which way's the bedroom?"

Sara was about to tell him when another contraction seized her. As she groaned, she pointed, hoping he'd understand.

"Hold on, Princess. Just hold on."

Chapter Twenty

Caleb knew something was wrong the moment he saw the strange Palomino. The horse waited patiently for whoever owned it, but the rider must've been in a hurry. He hadn't bothered to tether the animal.

After Caleb stopped his pair of horses, he jumped out of the wagon. "See to the horses?" he asked Ty as he headed toward the house.

"I got 'em." Ty climbed out of his saddle and tied up his Bay.

With a nod, Caleb marched toward the porch. His spade was lying next to the flowerbed Sara wanted to plant come spring, and it looked as though she'd been trying to dig it up. He'd have to scold her for overdoing just as soon as he found her.

Who did the damned Palomino belong to?

Something caught his gaze. A pink puddle of water not far from where she'd dropped the spade. His breath froze in his lungs. A moment later a frightened bellow spilled from his lips. "Sara!"

Sprinting up the porch steps, Caleb headed right through the front door, which was ajar. He jerked his gun from his holster. There were sounds coming from the bedroom, so he ran toward it. All sorts of scenes were rapidly playing through his thoughts. Rape. Murder. He kicked the door open to find his wife lying on the bed with a blond man leaning over her, his hands in her hair.

Caleb took aim, but Ty's hand came down hard on his arm. "Don't."

The blond glanced their way, and fear was plain in his eyes. "She's hurt."

Although nothing was what Caleb had expected, he recognized one thing.

Sara needed him.

Handing his gun to Ty, Caleb stripped his coat, dropping it on the floor. The blond smartly moved away from the bed before Caleb could shove him out of the way.

"Caleb. You're here." She reached for him, her voice tremulous.

Caleb took one look and wanted to shout his anger. The baby was coming. That much was clear. Her skirts were stained with the same pinkish water he'd seen outside. A large red stain marked the quilt under her. There was more blood than he could've imagined—more blood than he thought there should've been. "Oh, Sara... What happened?"

She groped for his hand. "Caleb. I'm so sorry. I slipped on the ice... I fell hard. My water broke and then my labor began."

"She's got a gash on the back of her head too," the man added. "I was trying to clean it and see if she needed some stitching up."

"Get the box, Caleb," Sara ordered before she frowned. "I–I fear I've ruined your mama's quilt. Please forgive me."

He let out a rueful chuckle. The woman was in danger and all she could worry about was a blanket. "It's okay, sweetheart."

"I'm sorry, Cal—" Her face contorted as she rolled to her side and pulled up her knees.

"Shh..." I'm here now." Looking over his shoulder, he barked an order to Ty. "Go get your wife and Grace Morgan. Tell 'em the baby's coming." Then he glared at the blond. "Get the box full of linens from the pantry."

"Where's the pantry?" the man asked.

"In the goddamn kitchen. Go!"

"It's too early," Ty replied.

"You think I don't know that?" Caleb snapped.

"It hurts, Caleb," Sara closed her eyes and bit hard on her bottom lip.

"I know, sweetheart." He gave Ty one more order. "Get a basin of water before you go."

The blond came skidding into the room, carrying the wooden box Sara had prepared that was full of linens—sheets, towels, twine, scissors—things she would need for the birth.

Caleb smoothed his hand over Sara's forehead as he glared at the man. "Who the hell are you?"

Before he could reply, Ty came back with a full basin. He walked so fast, water sloshed over the sides.

"Put it on the nightstand." Caleb fished a washing cloth from the box. After he dipped it in the water, he folded it and laid it over Sara's forehead.

She let out a long breath and opened her eyes. "Better now."

"Good," Caleb said with a nod. "Now I can see to that goose egg on your head."

"I hit it on a rock."

"I'm so sorry, sweetheart."

Ty grabbed the blond's arm. "This is Drake, a friend from Denver. I'll explain later. He's going with me to fetch the women. We can ride double and get 'em here fast as lightning."

The blond had cocked his head and was staring at Ty as though the man had gone daft.

There wasn't time for Caleb to ponder whether Ty was giving him the truth. Right now, the women needed to be dragged back here. Quickly. "Go!"

***

Sara was glad her head didn't need stitched. Caleb gently cleaned away the blood, pronounced the wound minor, and then helped her braid her hair. He'd also helped her out of her wet skirts and got her into a nightgown. In between, her labor pains came and went. The bleeding had stopped, which she prayed was a good sign. But beneath that hope was icy cold fear because one thing was plain to both of them.

The baby was coming too soon.

There were so many things she needed to tell him. About Drake. About the money. About what she'd been in her other lifetime.

Her time to explain things to him was running out. Surely Ty and Drake would be back with Cassie and Grace soon. She had to say something. Now.

Another contraction came upon her, making her suck in a ragged breath. The strength of each new pain increased, and her body wasn't in her control any longer. She could no more have stopped herself from straining to push the baby from her belly than she could've stopped the sun from setting.

"I don't think you should push so hard, sweetheart." Caleb laid the wet cloth over her forehead. "You should wait until Grace and Cassie get here to help."

She grunted out that she couldn't help it. Then the strangest sensation appeared in her core. "Oh, God... Caleb. I think...I think the baby's coming."

"Shit." He threw aside the sheet that covered her and laid a hand on her thigh. "I–I need to look down there. Okay?"

While she wanted to scream at him to hurry the hell up, she just groaned out a "yes."

He gently spread her thighs and gasped. "You're right, Sara. I can see the head."

"Too soon," she ground out between clenched teeth.

"We ain't got a choice." Grabbing for a few of the towels from the box, he jerked the sheet completely off the bed and crawled up on the mattress to deliver their child.

The contraction had no sooner ended when another one enveloped her. Sara let out a harsh cry and pushed with all her might. Her secrets would have to wait for another time. She had a job to do that simply couldn't be postponed.

Caleb saw the crown of dark hair emerging and swallowed hard. He was going to have to deliver this baby. There was no one else.

His hand trembled as he caught the infant's head when it emerged, cradling the neck as Sara struggled to push the baby's shoulders through her birth canal. A moment later, she succeeded, and he suddenly wished he had four hands. "It's a boy!"

The baby was blue, slippery, and his face was covered with thick mucus and membrane, much like a foal's would be. Caleb scrambled to hold the tiny, slick child while he wiped away anything that could be blocking the nose and mouth. Still, there was no cry of life. The baby was so small—tinier than any he'd ever seen before. He could cradle most of the body in his big calloused hands, and he feared his new son had arrived in the world too early to survive.

"No... Please." He kept daubing as much away from the baby's face as he could, then he pinched the nostrils, squeezing out fluid from each side and then wiping up the mess.

"Caleb... He's not crying." Sara let out a weak sob as she struggled to push herself up on her elbows. "He's not crying. Help him!"

"C'mon, little guy." Caleb worked frantically, dipping his finger in his son's mouth to scoop out anything that could obstruct a clean first breath. More and more mucus kept coming out, but no cry came forth in response.

Frustrated to the point tears blurred his vision, Caleb offered up a prayer for help as he tried one last desperate measure. He'd once helped a mare deliver a foal that had refused to breathe. The owner finally blew hard into the colt's nostrils to try to make the lungs fill and hopefully learn their job. The action must have dislodged whatever had kept that animal from taking its first breath. With the last of his hope, Caleb put his mouth over the boy's nose and mouth and tried to blow some air into the tiny lungs.

With a loud gasp, the baby sucked in his father's breath and then let out a wail worthy of a carnival barker.

Sara began to cry in earnest, collapsing back against the pillows. "Thank God. Thank God." Her words disappeared in gasps and sobs.

"Sara?" Cassie's voice echoed through the house.

No sound—other than his new son's cries—could be as sweet. "We're in here!" Caleb shouted back, making the baby cry louder.

Cassie and Grace came rushing into the bedroom, both in the process of shedding their heavy coats. As the infant kept crying, the women smiled.

"We missed all the fun," Cassie said.

"Fun?" Caleb had to snort at that. "You got a strange idea of fun, Cassie Bishop."

Grace picked up one of the flannel blankets, laid it over her arms, and held them out. "Give me the baby, Caleb. Let me get him cleaned up and wrapped tight against the cold."

The hesitation to give the little boy to Grace was a surprise. This was his son. Caleb had helped his wife bring him into the world, and now his purpose in life was to protect the boy. He seemed to have major difficulty giving him to another's care.

"Please, Caleb. Sara needs us. So does your son."

Gently, he laid the baby in Grace's arms. "Take good care of 'em both."

"You did well," she replied. Then she started barking orders at Cassie. "Get the twine and scissors. We've got to tie off the cord."

Coming closer to Sara, Caleb smoothed the damp wisps of hair away from her temples. "You done good, Sara."

Her eyes were closed, but he knew she'd heard because she smiled at his words.

"You tired?"

This time, she scoffed. "Perhaps a little." Her eyes opened, and the joy he saw reflected in those blue pools made his heart sing. "A *lot*."

"A girl," he whispered.

"What?"

Caleb pressed a kiss to her forehead. "Next time, we'll have a girl for you."

Chapter Twenty-One

His step light, a smile plastered on his face, Caleb grabbed a clean shirt and headed to the bathroom to wash up. His son's appearance had been messy, but after assisting in the birth of every breed of farm animal, he wasn't concerned. Birth was dirty business. That's all there was to it.

After he'd cleaned up and changed, he headed outside to talk to Ty and this Drake character. Caleb's anger at a stranger coming to his house had dimmed considerably since it was clear the man had helped Sara after she'd fallen. But there was still the mystery of what Drake wanted and why he'd come to the farm in the first place.

Caleb didn't recognize him, and Sara had been too indisposed to let him know whether she knew the man or not.

Time to find out for myself.

The chill hit him, but he'd left his heavy coat in the bedroom. He knew the women needed time to help Sara through the equally messy afterbirth chores, so he'd left well enough alone and walked outside in his shirt sleeves.

Drake leaned back against one of the posts, smoking a cheroot, while Ty paced the length of porch and back again. Both stared at Caleb when he cleared his throat loudly.

"How's Sara?" Ty asked, his voice anxious.

"Your sister's fine."

"The baby?"

From the time Caleb had met Ty, there'd been an undeclared war between them over who could better the other. When Ty had won Cassie's heart, Caleb took a long time getting past the defeat. Then Sara had come into his life, a way of God opening a window when he'd closed a door.

This time, Caleb could do a little nose-rubbing and not feel the worse for it.

"Baby's fine," Caleb said proudly. "Where *you* missed the chance, *I* was able to put the stem on the apple."

Ty's brow furrowed. "What in the hell does *that* mean?"

Drake was the one to reply. "Means he had a boy. I take it you've got a girl, right?" He shook his head and chuckled.

The time for niceties had ended. "Who are you?" Caleb asked.

After he pushed away from the post, Drake walked to the edge of the porch boards and tossed aside the last of his cheroot. It bounced into the frozen flower bed that Sara had been trying to dig up. "Drake Myers."

"Why did you come to my farm?"

"I was searching for someone," Drake replied. His gaze caught Caleb's. "A woman I knew as Princess."

"Princess?" Caleb snorted. "Damn stupid name if you ask me." Then the wording of Drake's statement registered. "*Was* looking? You found her then?"

"Yep."

The meaning was clear. "My wife sure as shit ain't called Princess."

"She was my Princess."

"You're full of shit," Caleb said with a dismissive wave of his hand.

Ty's reaction came as a surprise. "He's right."

"Right? That Sara was his Princess?" Another snort slipped out. "You two been hittin' the whiskey?"

"Caleb..." Ty let out a heavy sigh. "There's some things you should know 'bout Sara."

Caleb shook his head. "Anything Sara wants me to know, she's already told me."

"You didn't know she was Princess," Drake said, a sarcastic inflection to his voice.

All Caleb could think was that her old lover had given her that nickname and somehow this man had learned about it. That bastard Jean-Claude had used her and then dumped her like so much trash. It was easy to see a man like that calling her "Princess" as an exercise in irony. "Don't rightly care what that French son-of-a-bitch called her."

Pulling his lips to a grim line, Ty shook his head. "It weren't Jean-Claude called her that." He doffed his hat and raked his fingers through his thick hair. "Caleb, Sara got put into a place called The Palace."

All of the joy over the birth of his son was fading fast as Caleb began to understand the things Sara had hinted at but never found the courage to tell him. *The Palace.* He somehow doubted that was the name of a theater or an opera house.

"Go on," he ground out between his gritted teeth. "Tell me all of it." His hands ached from clenching them into tight fists.

"Jean-Claude—" Ty spit over the railing as though the name was bitter in his mouth, "—sold Sara to a lady named Crazy Kate."

"Kate ain't no *lady*," Drake countered. "She's a whore who runs The Palace."

Caleb took a threatening step toward Drake. "Are you calling my wife a whore?"

"I am."

When he pulled his fist back, ready to bury it in Drake's smug face, Caleb found his arm restrained by his brother-in-law. "You can't hit him for tellin' the truth, Caleb."

The truth?

What exactly *was* the truth?

Caleb didn't know anymore.

"She's a *whore*, and she's also a *thief*," Drake added. He appeared calm, but the taunt and the threat were there in his eyes.

This time, Ty couldn't hold Caleb back any more than a lady's fancy fan could've stopped a tornado. Since Ty held tight to Caleb's right arm, Caleb swung with his left, a blow Drake barely sidestepped.

Caleb jerked away from Ty and went after Drake again, fists swinging. He connected a right to Drake's nose, taking satisfaction in hearing the crack of bone.

Drake retaliated with a punch to the gut that forced the air from Caleb's lungs and had him doubled over, gasping and gagging.

"Enough!" Ty stepped between them, shoving Drake back with both hands and then facing Caleb. "He's only speakin' the truth. Sara had no choice. That bastard sold her like a damn slave to a bitch everyone calls Crazy Kate, who made her work as a whore. I found Sara not long after—a month, maybe—and tried to get her out. Didn't have the money. I came back here to try to gather enough, and I told my sister to get the hell outta there just as soon as she could."

Drake had jerked a handkerchief from his pocket and held the wadded cloth against his bleeding nose. "She stole my money. My whole fucking payroll. I lost my job 'cause of her. I'm getting that money back so people don't keep thinkin' I stole it. Ain't no one who'll hire me. I was a foreman, damn it!"

"She must've hightailed it right outta Denver," Ty added. "She showed up here not long after I left her there."

"And you did, didn't you?" Caleb glared at Ty. "Your own damn sister and you left her in a whorehouse!"

"I tried, Caleb. I swear to God I did. Kate ain't called Crazy for no reason. She's a mean bitch, and she had me thrown out when she realized I didn't have enough to buy Sara for the night, let alone enough to free her. Kate's got a big brute of a man working there who lifted me like I weighed nothin' and tossed me onto the street. All I could do was come back here and try to borrow the money from Adam Morgan."

"She stole it from me instead," Drake insisted. Every word he uttered sounded like they were spoken by a man with a wicked head cold.

Serves him right. Hope that nose hurts like hell.

Setting his hands against his hips, Caleb waited until he could breathe properly again. His mind raced a million different directions.

He loved Sara. Yet she'd lied to him. Repeatedly.

When she claimed she loved him, was that a lie? The kind of lie a whore told to keep getting money?

But they had a child. A son. She was his *wife*.

"One more thing," Drake said, although the hesitant tone was bewildering. "About that baby... Um... I was...with Princess..." He spit out some blood. "I slept with the woman the night she stole the payroll. That was about eight months ago."

Caleb closed his eyes against the pain, an agony that made Drake's punch feel like the touch of a light breeze. This time his heart had been hit with the staggering blow.

That baby boy, the one Caleb had breathed life into, might belong to another man.

And at that moment, he hated her as he'd hated no other person on the face of the earth.

In all the time he'd known her—had been married to her—Sara hadn't bled. Not once. There was a slim chance her monthly had come on the trip from Denver to White Pines, but something told him it hadn't. There would be no way to know whether the child was his or Drake's.

The baby's hair had been coal black, a shade darker than Sara's, resembling Caleb's black hair more than Drake's light brown. But that didn't mean anything. Grace Morgan had light brown hair too, and her son's was blond, often looking white when it lightened in the summer sun. Color was fickle to say the least...

The boy's eyes had been an odd shade of gray. Caleb had heard babies' eyes changed color as they grew. He didn't even know what color Drake's eyes were, nor did he give a shit at that moment.

All he knew was that his life was over, the life he'd thanked his Maker for, again and again.

A lie.

It's all a goddamn lie!

"Caleb..." Ty took a step closer.

Caleb growled like an angry bear and shoved Ty. "You son of a bitch. You knew. You *knew!* Why didn't you tell me?"

The fact Ty could stay so calm while Caleb's world was crumbling around him only turned his anger into white hot rage. "You and Sara had already married before I even knew she'd made it to town," Ty replied. "While you two were taking vows, I was tryin' to talk to Adam about the money Crazy Kate wanted for Sara."

At least that explanation made sense and kept Ty from being a part of this mess, other than he was the reason Sara had stumbled into Caleb's life in the first place. But Ty hadn't set Caleb up to take this fall.

Sara had.

Cassie came to the doorway and cast a furtive glance at Ty. "I'm sorry to interrupt..."

Ty's whole demeanor changed as he tossed his wife a smile. "It's okay, Cassie girl. What'cha want?"

"Sara is asking for Caleb."

***

Something was very wrong.

The moment Caleb stepped into their bedroom, Sara saw the change in him. His face was flushed, his hands held in tight fists. The softness and love in his eyes had vanished, and he breathed so hard his nostrils flared.

"I–I thought you'd like to see our son," she said. She'd waited until Grace and Cassie had helped clean everything up. Now she was washed, dressed in a clean nightgown, and sitting on a mound of pillows. She was sore, tired, and in desperate need of sleep, but she wanted to share this important moment with the man she loved.

Caleb arched a dark eyebrow. "Is he?"

"Is he what?"

"Our son."

"Caleb, what on earth—?"

"*Our* son." A rueful, haunting laugh tumbled from his lips. "Yours. That's for damn sure. Since I caught him in my own hands, I can vouch for that. But mine?" Another chilling chuckle. "*That* might be a problem."

Her heart skipped a beat before it jumped to a furious cadence. "Caleb... I..." The words wouldn't come. She wasn't sure whether to confess or beg for his forgiveness, but one thing was crystal clear.

Drake had spilled the news.

She could hear him now, his voice echoing in her mind as he told Caleb that she'd serviced him like any good whore, plied him with strong whiskey, and then robbed him blind while he slept off his bender. Somehow Caleb had also put two and two together to arrive at the conclusion that Drake could have fathered the precious, impossibly tiny boy sleeping in her arms.

Tears burned her eyes, but she tried to hold tight to her emotions. All the tears in the world wouldn't fix this. The only thing she could do was tell Caleb the truth—not Drake's version, which made her appear a sinner of epic proportions, but the honest tale of how Jean-Claude had turned her into something she simply wasn't.

I'm not a whore.

I'm not.

"Come and see your son." She kissed the baby's forehead. "He's *your* son, Caleb Young."

"Another lie to add to the pile of lies that bastard just buried me in."

"You won't even listen to me? You won't let me explain?"

"How can you *explain* working at The Palace?"

"I was sold to The Palace. I had no choice!"

"Another lie."

"I never lied to you! I tried to tell you," she insisted. "You said the past didn't matter."

"Bullshit." He ran his hand over his face. "I married a lie."

"You married a *woman*. Me. I'm sorry I'm not what you expected." She closed her eyes as she realized exactly what her husband wasn't saying. "You *think* you know what I am. But you don't."

"How could you lie to me? How could you keep lying to me? Over and over and over..."

"Caleb, please. Give me chance."

"You should've told me you were a...a..." With a shake of his head he glanced away.

"You can't even say it, can you?" Sara stared at him, watching her future burning into nothing but a pile of ashes. "Say it, Caleb." Her raised voice set her son to squirming.

Caleb shook his head again.

Had she seen tears—any sign that his feelings hadn't died—she might have begged for forgiveness or tried harder to explain. But when his gaze found hers again, all she saw was white hot hatred.

He would never listen to her. Ever. He'd already made up his mind.

The truth had killed his love...assuming he'd ever really loved her at all.

She simply didn't know.

It was her fault for putting Caleb Young on a pedestal, for thinking he was different than all the other men she'd known.

But he wasn't.

He'd wanted her for the same reason Jean-Claude had. The same reason her customers had. She was a woman who offered them a warm body, a chance to rut like an animal. To fuck.

And that was all she and Caleb had shared. Some nice fucks.

"Say it," she said again, her voice full of hurt and disappointment as their son began to wail.

"Sara..."

This time, she shouted the command. "Say it!"

"You are a whore."

Not *you were. You are.*

Sara refused to hang her head. "I am what the world made me, what Jean-Claude made me."

Caleb stomped over to door and practically ripped it off the hinges.

Then he left, slamming the door behind him.

Chapter Twenty-Two

The company wasn't at all unexpected, even if it was uninvited.

Caleb let out a sigh. Hanging up the last of the skins, he waited until the horse and rider drew close enough for him to see who'd come to scold him. Turned out his older brother had the honors. Hell, he was amazed Gideon had waited four full weeks to hunt him down.

Gideon's stern expression did little to ease the anger that still bubbled deep inside Caleb's heart and soul. Funny, but that anger shifted, even on an hourly basis.

Sometimes it was directed at Sara. His lawful wife.

Or was she his lawful wife?

Surely the marriage could be set aside on the grounds of her deception. Not only had she lied to him, she'd might have come to the marriage pregnant with another man's child. She was a whore—and a thief as well. There had to be legal precedent aplenty for him to obtain an annulment. If not an annulment, then a divorce.

What did he have to lose at this point? His pride? His standing in the community?

Sara.

He would lose Sara.

Why did he still love her so damned much? And why did some of his anger at her often shift to himself?

That rage was the hardest to handle. When Caleb could blame Sara for this mess, he didn't have to acknowledge that he'd walked out on his wife and newborn son. They hadn't even had a chance to baptize the boy or give him a name, and Caleb had waltzed right out the door without so much as a fare-thee-well.

What kind of monster did something like that?

"Brother." Gideon inclined his head. "You're looking fit as ever. I reckon I gave you long enough to lick your wounds, so I'm here to talk some sense into you."

"Say what you need to say, then get outta here. I've got work to do."

Gideon's gaze went to the long line of animal furs. "So I see. What'cha gonna do with all those?"

"What do you think, numb nuts? Sell 'em. A man's gotta eat."

"Seems to me you should have plenty of meat."

The joke fell flat. "How'd you find me, Gideon?"

"Weren't difficult," Gideon replied as he climbed out of the saddle. He took off his hat and hooked it over the saddle horn. "Where else you got to go? Knew the cabin would be the perfect place for you to pout."

"I ain't pouting!"

"'Brood' work any better for you? How about 'mope'? They're all mighty fitting."

"Gideon, I ain't up to your lectures. Go on home." Turning his back, Caleb stalked into the sparse cabin.

The walls were closing in on him. For the last month, he'd lived in the one-room trapping cabin he and Gideon had built years ago when they found out how profitable fur sales were. Wolf pelts fetched the best prices, but hunting them was difficult and tedious. Good thing Caleb had so much time on his hands, even if each minute ticked by as though it were an hour.

How was Sara? How was that tiny boy? Had she recovered from the ordeal of birth? Was she still on their farm, working to get her flower bed planted?

Or had she left? Had she given up on their marriage and joined Drake to scurry back to Denver? He was, after all, her last customer. Didn't she have to feel affection for a man to sleep with him? She'd certainly done a great job seducing Caleb into her bed, reacting as though she enjoyed his touch when it had probably been an act— nothing but a show. Had she performed as well for Drake? For all the other men she'd slept with?

He shook his head to try to banish the images and strode to the table to grab the whiskey that was now in short supply. Although it was close to empty, he wrapped his fingers around the bottle and lifted it to his lips. Then he drank, letting the whiskey blaze a fiery path down his throat as he waited for the wonderful forgetting that came with each swallow.

"Tryin' to drink her away?" Gideon's heavy footfalls echoed on the floorboards. "Ain't gonna work, you know."

After finishing the last of the amber liquid, Caleb slammed the bottle on the table. "Go home. Go back to Drew, and stay the hell outta my life."

"She's barely getting by."

"What's that s'posed to mean?"

"She's trying to keep the farm running while she's nursing your baby and—"

"He ain't mine!"

"The hell he ain't! You forget, little brother, I saw you not more than ten minutes after you came outta our mama's womb. That baby is your spittin' image. Your seed made him. He's your son."

If only he could believe that...

With a loud snort, Caleb headed right back outside. Gideon couldn't know the torment he was living with every day, every hour, every minute. His love for his wife warred with his hate, and neither side was winning. Like most battles, the worst of the damage was to the battlefield, which was, in this case, his heart.

He felt a hundred years old.

"He's Drake's son," Caleb said, not at all surprised his brother was trailing him like a shadow.

"She's gonna make herself sick, Caleb."

That got his attention. He glared at his brother. "Sick?"

"She won't eat. She won't sleep. She's running herself into the ground. Got it in her head she needs the farm to be exactly as it was when you left without a lick of help. Won't touch the money I offer her. No way a woman on her own can handle all that, 'specially one with a newborn at her breast."

Although his heart was full of sympathy and worry, Caleb stood his ground. "Tell her to hire some help."

"With what? Told you she won't take my money, and you didn't leave her a plugged nickel."

Caleb scoffed. "She knows how to make money. Tell her to spread her thighs and—"

He never saw the blow coming. And what a punch it was. Gideon's fist connected with Caleb's face, sending lights flashing behind his eyes.

Dropping to his knees, Caleb gently tested his aching jaw. "What'cha go and do that for?"

"To shut your fool mouth. Sara ain't a whore. Didn't you hear anything she told you? She ain't a whore. She was a damn slave. Didn't have a choice in it. She was just trying to survive."

If only he could accept that. If only he could banish the images of her sweet body wrapped around Drake and other faceless customers.

How many? Dozens? Hundreds?

He was a man tormented.

As he dragged himself to his feet, Caleb realized a trip to town would have to come soon. He was running out of whiskey. But he'd skip going near his home. Only once in the month since he'd left the farm had he ventured close. From the top of the tallest hill, he'd waited in the trees, watching for a sign of Sara, any sign. After an hour, she'd come from the house, carrying the well-bundled baby against her shoulder.

The moment he saw her, regret had choked him. Without a moment's hesitation, he'd reined his horse south and headed to White Pines, glad there was no chance of running into her. That trip had been quick and perfunctory, and Caleb had been blessed with few questions and no glimpse of people who'd demand an explanation. He'd loaded up on whiskey and vital supplies and hightailed it right back to the trapping cabin.

Gideon shook out his fingers as if the punch had hurt him as well. "You're a damned fool. You've got a wife who loves you more than life, a son who needs a father, and here you are. Drinking yourself stupid."

"Go away, Gideon. I ain't going back." When Caleb tried to get to his feet, Gideon kicked him hard in the seat of his pants. He tumbled into the dust. "Stop it."

"When you stop sayin' ridiculous things. God, I want to beat you 'til you're a stain on the ground."

"Couldn't if you wanted to."

"Don't tempt me." Gideon scowled at him for a few long moments before he shook his head. "Wouldn't do no good anyway. You're too damn stubborn. Take some advice from someone older and wiser. Get yourself home, Caleb. Before it's too late."

"It's already too late. I'm thinkin' a divorce—" That earned him another swift kick in the backside. Caleb fell forward, his face slamming into the dirt.

With a heavy sigh, he rolled over and propped himself up with an elbow. "Stop it!"

"Already told you...quit sayin' dumb things and I will. Did you forget all about our mama?"

Caleb froze. He *had* forgotten. He'd been so lost in self-pity over losing faith in his wife he'd pushed all the tales of how his father had rescued his mother from the same kind of life Sara lived.

But that was his mother. That was another lifetime ago.

Sara was his *wife*.

"What do you want from me?" he asked, rubbing his hand over his sore jaw and pushing aside truths he didn't want to acknowledge.

"I want you to go home and tell that woman—that woman you love—that you've forgiven her."

"But I ain't forgiven her. I can't!" Caleb wasn't sure he even *could*. She'd betrayed him in a way he wasn't sure he would ever find a way to forgive.

She'd broken his heart.

Gideon swept his hat on his head and threw himself into the saddle. He glared down at Caleb as though he dearly wanted to punch him a few more times. "Get your ass home, Caleb. Before she gives up and leaves."

On that, he prodded his horse and trotted away.

"Good riddance!" Caleb shouted.

His brother's response was to keep riding, glance over his

shoulder, and shake his head.

***

The rooster had started crowing before the sun was even up.

Sara watched the noisy cock saunter around the yard, flaunting his feathery body and bright crimson comb, and considered having him for Sunday dinner simply to get some peace and quiet. She dropped the rest of the chicken feed from her apron onto the ground, trying not to step on any of the chickens frantically scratching and pecking for their breakfast. Judging from the number of eggs she'd gathered this morning and the bevvy of new chicks filling the coop, the noisy cock was inspiring the hens, so he was safe. For another day.

Who knew what tomorrow would bring?

After closing the coop's gate behind her, Sara leaned back against one of the posts, wiped her forehead with the back of her long sleeve, and sighed. All she wanted to do was close her eyes and sleep for the rest of the day. But there was work to be done. Plenty of work—more than she could truly handle on her own.

But the farm needed to keep running. It was the only way Caleb would ever forgive her—if she saved his farm.

She needed his help. The work was backbreaking for only one person, especially a woman who had to stop often to nurse a greedy baby. Most of the time, she cradled her son against her chest in a sling Drew had helped her fashion. The child would know everything there was about milking cows, gathering eggs, and tilling a garden before he could walk, because he was there as his mother completed each of those chores.

Sometimes Drew and Gideon would come by to lend a hand, but they had plenty to do in their own world. Drew would be acting in a play soon and was kept busy with constant rehearsals. Gideon had his own planting and milking to complete. No matter how desperately she needed help, she wouldn't ask them to sacrifice their valuable time.

This was *her* quest—her white whale to harpoon, as the Melville book would claim.

She only hoped her ending was more favorable than poor Captain Ahab's.

She glanced over to the wooden box resting on the porch. Needing to keep a close eye on her boy, Sara had created a cradle from an old peach crate. All she'd needed was to pad it well with blankets, and the baby could sleep in it anywhere she needed to take him. Since the weather had finally taken a turn for the warmer, it was easy to keep the child close at hand by keeping him in the crate rather than in the sling.

Although he was still tiny, he was gaining height and weight rapidly. That slight weight, even when supported against her chest, stole more and more of her waning strength.

The baby. My son. The child. He deserved better. He deserved a name.

Sara no longer doubted that he was Caleb's son. Everything about him screamed the fact. It helped that Gideon went on and on about how much the baby looked like Caleb, something that was easy to see with her own eyes. But to hear that the boy was the mirror image of Caleb as a baby helped. A lot.

Not that it mattered a lick to her. She loved the boy with every ounce of her heart and soul. He gave her a reason to rise each morning and to keep putting one foot in front of the other.

Thinking she'd honor her son with the same name as Caleb's father, she asked Gideon for the name. When he'd chuckled and told her, she'd quickly discarded that idea. She wasn't about to name her son Nebuchadnezzar. At first she thought Gideon was simply pulling her leg, so he'd shown her the family Bible to prove it. The name was scrawled there in big, bold letters.

The man's middle name had caught her eye. *Isaac.* More and more she began to think of the baby as Isaac.

She went to the boy, bent down, and kissed his chubby cheek. A smile, one of the first ones she'd managed in the long month, crossed her lips. "Isaac Young. I do believe from today forward, you will be Isaac Young. Your papa can pick a middle name. Serves him right for staying away so long." To that declaration she gave a decisive nod.

The sound of hoof beats made her glance to the east. A single rider was approaching.

Sara reached to the small of her back and pulled Caleb's revolver from where it had rested in her waistband. She was so vulnerable out here, all alone. Her son needed her protection.

Isaac. Isaac needed her protection.

Squinting against the sunlight, she breathed a sigh of relief that she recognized the rider.

Drake was back.

He stopped his horse close to the barn, dismounted, and came marching across the yard with the cockiness of that pesky rooster. The same determined frown he'd offered on his other two visits was fixed on his face. He tipped the brim of his hat. "Mornin', Miss Sara."

Putting the gun back into her waistband, she frowned. "I told you, Drake. I don't want you here. I don't need help. Not from you." *Not from anyone...*

With a heavy sigh, he jerked his hat from his head and threaded his fingers through his hair. "I just wanna help." His gaze drifted around the farm. "You could use some muscle. The fence needs mending. The garden needs more tilling."

"Those tasks are both on my list." The long list of things she needed to get done as quickly as possible. Mentally, she moved the garden up to the first slot. The springs and summers in Montana were short, to say the least. She needed to get all the seedlings Grace and Cassie had brought her planted in the garden.

But if she didn't get the fence mended, the cows were likely to wander. Perhaps that should be the first item on her list...

"The money's back in Denver," Drake said, flopping his hat back on his head.

Her eyes fixed on the flower bed. It was still a mess from where she'd had Drake dig up what was left of the payroll. Thanks to the cash Caleb kept under the mattress, she was able to add enough to replace most of what she'd used to travel from Denver to Montana. His former boss had accepted payment and cleared Drake's name and reputation.

Which begged the question, "Why are you still here?" Since Isaac had begun to fuss, Sara picked him up and held him to her chest. He'd want nursed soon, and her breasts were full and ready. She just had to get rid of Drake first. "Go on home."

"I can't leave you like this, Miss Sara. Not after... Please let me help. It's the only way I'll ever shed this guilt."

"You have nothing to feel guilty about," she insisted.

He shook his head. "I got plenty."

Isaac was latching onto her bodice. "Please. Just go. I don't need your help." She mounted the porch steps. "I don't need anyone.

Except Caleb...

***

"What in the devil?" Sara took one look at Drake working on the fence and lost her temper.

She set a fed, burped, and now content Isaac in his makeshift cradle and stomped out to confront Drake. "Are you deaf?"

"Being as your hollering just made my ears ring, I'd say no, ma'am."

"Then perhaps you're merely hard of hearing."

He shook his head, but his lips twitched into a grin. He stuck a couple of nails between his lips, held one against the rail, and pounded it in with the hammer.

"Don't you dare smile at me, Drake...um... What is your last name anyway?"

"Myers, ma'am. Drake Myers."

"Then listen here, Mr. Myers. I told you to get off my farm."

Instead of replying, he hammered the rest of the nails into the post, finishing the work the fence needed. Although she was grateful the difficult task was complete, she found it grating that not only had he done it, he'd done it so easily. All he'd needed was the time she'd taken to change and feed her son.

Drake hung the hammer on his belt and picked up the glass Caleb used to store nails. "Stop letting your pride take the lead."

"I beg your pardon?"

He leveled a stare at her, his brown eyes full of pity she didn't care to see. "You need help, but you're too damn prideful to accept it."

"My pride has nothing to do with it."

His scoffing laugh made her want to slap his face. "You can't do this all by yourself. Let me help, at least 'til your husband comes back."

"I can do it alone."

Drake reached for her hand and cradled it in his. "No, Miss Sara. You can't."

She tried to tug her hand back, he wouldn't let go. "Why can't you just leave me alone?"

"Because I'm the reason you're in this nasty fix."

"I–I stole your money." Her eyes blurred with unshed tears. She hadn't cried, not once since Caleb left. She wouldn't allow herself the luxury now, not matter how remorseful she felt over her confession. "You did nothing wrong."

"Didn't I? I came riding in here, screamin' for your head on a platter. I shoulda at least talked to you before shooting my mouth off." He let go of her hand. "I'm sorry I drove your husband off." He glanced back to where Isaac slept. "I cost that boy his daddy."

"He'll be back." Her voice held no conviction, because with each passing day her hopes fell a little more. "He'll be back." This time she gave him a nod, turned, and walked away.

Drake fell in step beside her. "Let me stay 'til then. Then I won't feel so damn guilty."

"I don't know..."

Moving quickly past her, he turned and caught her upper arms in his grasp. "Please. Do I gotta beg? Let me make this up to you."

"Why aren't you back in Denver?" she couldn't help but ask.

"Ain't nothing there for me. Besides," he said with a shrug, "I kinda like it here. It's...peaceful. Quiet. Tired of looking up the ass...um...backside of steers too. Only wish I had a roof over my head. At least I can see the big Montana sky while I'm bedded down."

Sara felt guilty all over again. Not only had she robbed the man, now he was sleeping out in the elements because he'd had to track her all the way out here. She owed him so much more than a rude dismissal.

Then the list—the far-too-long list—popped back into her head. She needed help, even if her pride would suffer by getting it. To that point, Drake was correct. Running this farm by herself was a matter of stubborn pride, the pride that had shattered the day her husband, the man she loved with all her heart and soul, called her a whore. Making the farm a success would help her regain some self-worth.

But would that restored pride vanish if she had someone working at her side?

"I'll pay you a small salary," she finally offered. "It's warm enough you can bed down in the loft of the barn. Take it or leave it."

His smile was so broad, his white teeth sparkled in the sunlight. "I'll take it."

Chapter Twenty-Three

The red fox popped from its hiding place, startling Caleb. Then a smile bloomed as a memory floated back…

Sara had made it her goal to save her eggs from the crimson vixen that liked to hunt in the chicken coops. The animal never took the hens, only trotted away with a mouth full of eggs every time she slipped through the fence. In his mind's eye, Caleb saw a very pregnant Sara, armed with a broom, chasing the fox and threatening all sorts of dire consequences if it didn't drop her precious eggs.

"Sara! Did you just see that—?"

The smile fell to a frown.

How many times a day did he turn to his wife only to find himself alone? And how many times did that loneliness make his heart tighten and tears sting his eyes?

That bitter seclusion was what made him seek a bride in the first place. He'd been rewarded—*blessed*—with a woman he came to not only love but to like as well. He missed lying in bed with his wife and talking about their day or the plans they had for their future. Every single day was a gift to Sara, and their farm was paradise in her eyes. Caleb had begun to look at his life in a whole new way.

Thanks to Sara.

Gideon's visit had robbed him of sleep. Their mother's story first whispered and then shouted in Caleb's brain. She'd been a woman—a very young and frightened woman—alone in a rough place where there was no one she could turn to, no one to help her survive the harsh world. Just like Sara. His mother had survived by selling her body.

What kind of man had his father been to take a woman like that as his wife?

A good man.

A forgiving man.

The whiskey no longer drowned the pain, nor did it help Caleb forget her. Instead, she was in his every waking thought—and his dreams, too. He'd awaken in the wee hours, his senses filled with her scent and the feel of her soft skin. With his cock hard and aching, he'd reach for Sara only to grasp nothing but cold sheets.

Hiking back to the cabin, Caleb tried to revive the anger and hatred over the lies Sara had told. Each day, those emotions were getting harder and harder to grasp. They sluiced through his fingers like grains of sand, and they were being replaced by regret and the unending loneliness.

How was Sara? How was the baby? Asking himself those questions was fruitless, so he made up his mind. He needed to find out for himself. Not that he'd ever draw close enough to talk to her. He couldn't. If he did, he might forget her betrayal, take her into his arms, and never let her go.

Betrayal.

What an odd word. It implied she'd been disloyal to him. But everything she'd done that he blamed her for had happened before he'd even *met* her. More and more he considered how Sara had been thrown into choppy waters without anyone to help her. She'd had to face a "sink or swim" situation. From what Gideon had said, she hadn't wanted to work at The Palace. Far from it. She'd been no better than a slave. And she'd only stolen the money from Drake to escape that horror. Both explanations blunted the sharp edge of Caleb's pain.

After saddling and mounting his horse, he sat staring at the stark cabin for a long moment. He had a melancholy notion that it represented his heart. Cold and bare.

He couldn't stand looking at it a moment longer.

***

Another lonely day.

Sara was exhausted. When her stomach rumbled, it dawned on her she hadn't eaten supper the night before. There was simply too much to do to waste time eating.

She wanted to pull the covers over her head and pretend the world didn't exist. But that damned rooster wouldn't allow the luxury. Only a few moments after it set to crowing, Isaac's cries echoed through the house.

With a resigned sigh, she kicked aside the covers and padded her way to her son's cradle. "Good morning," she said as she leaned over and smiled down at him. "It sounds like someone is ready for breakfast."

After changing him and eating her own breakfast while he nursed, Sara set Isaac on the bed as she dressed. She never bothered with a corset any longer. There was so much bending and lifting during her day and the garment was just too confining. Besides...there was no one to impress. No one to look good for.

Sara braided her hair while Isaac noisily sucked on his fist. She grinned at his slurps. Her son was the only thing that could bring a smile to her lips. Every day he looked more and more like his father. Same hair. Same eyes. Same profile. She thanked God for that incredible resemblance. It allowed her to stop fretting over whose seed had created the beautiful baby boy. Not that it mattered to her... But it clearly did to Drake, who was also convinced the boy wasn't his.

Oh, how she wanted to share all of their son's changes with Caleb! Isaac smiled now, especially when she blew on his fat little belly. For a child so tiny at birth, he fattened up quickly and ate as though there were no tomorrow. Soon she'd have to add something heartier to Isaac's diet. Breast milk wouldn't be enough for the growing boy.

A tear fell from the corner of her eye, but she quickly swiped it away and straightened her spine. Each day that passed took a chip out of her hopes that her husband would return. Gideon had found Caleb and told Sara that her husband was well. She had no doubt Gideon had tried to talk Caleb into coming home. Clearly that discussion had been unsuccessful.

At first, she'd prayed the time alone would give him some clarity. Maybe when he was alone up there in that cabin he'd realize what he'd lost and decide to come back to her. And forgive her.

There was only one thing to do. Work harder. She'd have to show him what an asset she was. She would have to prove the farm meant every bit as much to her as it did to him.

And that's that.

When she stepped out on the porch, Drake was riding up the road. She had tried so many times to convince him she was fine. Unfortunately, he saw right through her pretense. There was just too much work for one person. But if she didn't keep the farm running by herself, would her efforts still atone for her sins? If they didn't, how would she ever get Caleb to come back to her?

Drake was grinning from ear to ear.

"You look like a fat cat who ate a bird, feathers and all," Sara said after he came over to tweak Isaac's nose, making the baby smile.

"Don't know about that," he drawled. "But got some news."

She set her son in the peach crate and then put her hands on her hips. "Out with it."

"I sold those calves for you."

As a way to raise the money she needed for a new windmill, Sara had asked Drake to make inquiries into selling the two calves. There were already plenty of milk cows, and one bull was all they needed. So despite the fact she was strongly attached to the babies she'd helped deliver, she needed the funds their sale would bring.

But was the money for the sale going to be enough?

"For how much?" she asked, holding her breath.

"Well, I know you've got your heart set on that new windmill...but..." He shook his head and glanced away.

"I don't *want* that windmill, Drake. I *need* that windmill." The egg money was good but not nearly enough for the supplies she'd need for construction. She'd gambled on selling the calves. They were about the only asset she could sell.

That thought made her frown. She'd used all the cash Caleb had in the cabin to pay back the funds she'd stolen. Although he'd told her he was rich, she didn't know where he kept his wealth, nor would she touch another penny, only taking what she needed to help pay back Drake. This predicament was entirely her fault.

Everything was her fault.

She hung her head.

Drake nudged her chin up with his finger. Then he grinned. "I got enough for your windmill."

Sara let out a happy squeal and threw herself into his arms, hugging him tightly. "Thank you. Thank you. Thank you."

An enraged bellow echoed from the hillside, the sound sending a chill racing the length of her body.

Drake quickly shoved her behind his back as a rider came charging down the steep slope, moving too fast for safety. Only when the horse reached the flat ground did Sara stop worrying about whether the daft man would break his neck or his horse's legs.

The rider let out another shout, and recognition made Sara dig her fingers into the back of Drake's vest. "It's Caleb."

"You're sure?"

"I'm sure."

When she tried to skirt around him, Drake pushed her back. "Well, I ain't sure it's safe."

"Safe? Of course it's safe. Caleb's my husband." She forced her way around Drake and hurried to pick up Isaac, ready to face her husband and finally have things out. But first, he needed to greet his son.

Drake came to stand at her side. As fast as Caleb was riding, she figured it was better if they stayed on the porch, worried he wouldn't be able to stop his charge and would trample them all.

"You bastard!" Caleb threw himself off his horse and hit the ground running. "Get your goddamn hands off my wife!" He launched himself up the stairs, wrapped his arms around Drake's waist, tackling him. They rolled around, dropping off the porch and landing with a thud on the grass.

The battling men became a tangle of arms and legs. Punches were thrown, and all Sara could do was scream for them to stop. Her shrieks made Isaac wail every bit as loudly.

Thank God, Ty chose that time to ride up the lane.

"Ty!" she hollered. "Hurry!"

Her brother prodded his horse into a gallop and made it to the house quickly. Not that it mattered to Caleb or Drake, they were still pounding each other, their spit, sweat, and blood flying in every direction.

"Sweet Jesus." Ty jumped off his horse and raced to the scuffling men. He tried several times to break them up. After getting hit himself a couple of times, he stepped back, drew his gun, and shot it in the air.

The terrifying sound had the proper effect. The fighting men jerked apart.

Ty grabbed Drake's collar to drag him farther away from Caleb, who knelt there glaring at them both as he tried to catch his breath.

"What in the hell is going on here?" Ty asked, his gaze shifting from Caleb to Drake and finally to Sara.

Caleb clenched his sore hands into tight fists, ready to go right back at the son-of-a-bitch who'd dared touch Sara. His rage was focused on Drake, yet he felt not a single bit of anger at his wife. She was a victim—had *always* been a victim—of circumstance.

Sara was a survivor.

Drake, on the other hand, was clearly taking advantage of her vulnerability at being out here all alone.

Struggling to his feet, Caleb narrowed his eyes at his rival. "Get up and fight like a man."

When Drake tried to rise, Sara stepped between them and leveled a threatening glare at Drake. "Stay down."

Without a word of dissent, Drake dropped back on his ass.

She whirled to face Caleb. "You... you..." After letting out a frustrated groan, she stomped to her brother, shoved the baby into his arms, and then opened the door. "Inside, Caleb. It's time for us to have a long talk."

Chapter Twenty-Four

Sara should have been wary of the storm in Caleb's eyes, but her heart was brewing one of its own. She would have her say, then she'd let him have his.

After that?

Only God knew what would happen to their marriage...

Caleb stood with his arms folded over his chest, his legs braced apart, as though he expected a fight. "What in the hell is that bastard doing here?"

"If you're referring to Drake, I hired him to be my handyman. I'm ashamed to admit it, but I needed some assistance to keep the farm running. I tried to do everything myself, but..." She shrugged then let out a frustrated, resigned sigh. "I simply couldn't do it alone, no matter how badly I wished I could."

"Handyman?" Caleb gave her a rude snort.

She didn't want to dance around the real issue, but it was taking every ounce of her strength not to rush to him, wrap her arms around him, and beg him to forgive her.

But forgive her for what?

In the time he'd been gone, Sara had come to terms with her past. She'd been dealt so many mortal blows, and she'd made a few terrible decisions. But in the end, all she'd done was try to survive. Surely Caleb had figured that out for himself, and if that was enough for him to condemn her, so be it.

She was stronger now. She was no longer a woman who was nothing but a victim of circumstances. And she had something to live for—*someone* to live for.

Isaac.

Although Isaac deserved a father, he also deserved a man who respected his mother. If Caleb couldn't manage that...

Then he wasn't the man she thought he was, the man she thought she'd married.

"Are you coming home to stay?" Her question ended with her voice breaking.

It had taken every bit of her courage to ask, but she needed to know. This wasn't how she'd planned his return. Not at all.

In her fantasies, he would ride up and greet her with a smile. He would take a good look around, see how she'd worked her fingers to the bone to keep the farm running, and tell her what a great job she'd done. His heart would be so full of gratitude that he'd jump from his horse, fall to knees, and beg her forgiveness for having left her in such a lurch—all alone with a newborn baby.

A fairy tale. But life wasn't a fairy tale, was it?

"I need to know Caleb." Sara tried to control the panic in her tone. This moment was pivotal. Life changing. If he couldn't accept her, faults and all, she would have to leave. There was no other choice. The farm belonged to him, no matter how much she wanted it to be her home for the rest of her life. "Are you home for good? Because if not..." With a sigh, she walked to the window, staring out at the hills as she wrapped her arms around herself. "Then I shall have to go."

"Answer me this, Sara," Caleb said, his voice rough. "Why is Drake here?"

"I told you he's—"

"I know what you *said.* Now I want to know the *real* reason. Did you bring him here?"

"Certainly not." The moments clicked by slowly before she realized exactly what he was asking. "He feels...guilty."

"Guilty?"

Sara turned back to face her husband, needing to see his reactions. If his love for her was dead—lost to her unfortunate past—then she wanted to see it for herself. "He blames himself."

"For what?"

"For coming here all angry and indignant, shouting accusations. He believes he made me lose my husband and Isaac lose his father."

He scrunched up his forehead. "Isaac?"

"Our son. I couldn't abide by him not having a name, so I gave him your father's."

Caleb cocked his head. "But Pa's name was Nebuchadnezzar ."

She tried not to smile at that ridiculous name. "And quite a mouthful that is. I did not wish to constantly misspell my own son's name, so I gave him your father's middle name. I'm sorry if that displeases you."

"I'm not...displeased." He jerked his hat off and tossed it on the table. His eyes captured hers. "I'm glad you didn't leave him without a name."

"It didn't seem right." It was hard to hold his gaze. There were so many emotions reflected in those brown eyes, but she couldn't put her finger on what he was feeling. "You still haven't answered my question. Are you home for good?"

"What if I ain't?"

"Pardon?"

"What will you do if I ain't coming home?"

This was a time for honesty. He had to understand exactly what he'd lose. "This is your farm, Caleb. If you don't wish to remain my husband, I will pack my things and go."

"Go? Go where?"

"To stay with Ty and Cassie for now. Then I shall..." *Find a job? Head to a big city?* "What does it matter? If you don't want me, if you want to end this marriage..." She had to resist stomping her foot like an angry child. "I thought you were my knight in shining armor," she whispered.

"A knight? What are you talking about?"

"Never mind. Just never mind."

A shudder raced through her. She'd worked so damned hard to show him she could be a good wife, that she was more than the baggage of her past. All he had to do was walk around the farm to see it. The animals were fed and well cared for. The garden was planted. Soon, the windmill would be in place. The only chore she hadn't completed was the flowerbed. For some reason, she couldn't bring herself to touch it, not as long as her husband wasn't home.

Why wouldn't he say anything?

"I won't apologize," Sara insisted when she couldn't stand the silence another second. "Not again. I did what I had to do. Can't you understand that? I would think you'd be more understanding, what with your mother's history and—"

He shook his head at her. "You ain't my mother."

"I never said I was. I simply meant that she'd found herself in similar...circumstances. Your father still married her. He still..." *...loved her.*

Perhaps that union had worked because Caleb's father truly loved his mother. Perhaps all of the declarations of love Caleb had given her were nothing but meaningless words.

Perhaps there was no hope for her future with the man she loved.

Still he stared, and she could take no more. "Will you please say something?"

Caleb held his tongue, afraid to answer. The moment he told her everything that was in his heart, he'd have to touch her. And the moment he touched her, he wouldn't be able to stop until he made love to her. But first, he would take advantage of how freely she spoke.

She was frustrated. Anxious. Those emotions made it harder for her to guard her words, and for the first time since they'd married, she was telling him the truth—the stark naked truth. He reveled in it, knowing honesty would be the only way they could put the past behind them and move forward.

Together.

All he'd needed to make him wise up was seeing Drake pull Sara into his embrace. In that moment, Caleb realized with blinding clarity that he still loved her—probably even loved her more for all she'd been through. Despite the way the world had mistreated her, she'd come out a caring woman, every bit as beautiful inside as out.

When Drake had dared to touch her, something primitive had seized the reins. Caleb wanted no other man to touch her! Ever! She belonged to him! She was his wife!

That's when he knew that nothing—past, present, or future—should keep them apart. They'd taken vows, promised to stay together through good times and bad until death parted them, and he intended to honor those pledges and to see that she did as well.

Tears spilled over her lashes. "It seems you have nothing to say to me, so nothing has changed. I will get my things together. I'll need to gather a few things for Isaac, too."

"You ain't going anywhere," he snapped.

She gaped at him before shaking her head. "I am. I have to go. I won't stay with a man who doesn't love me."

Caleb hurried to her and wrapped his arms around her. He was surprised she struggled, but he held tight, even as she slapped as his chest and started crying in earnest.

"Let me go," she insisted.

"Never," he replied, his voice husky with emotion. "I'll never let you go."

She stopped fighting and looked up at him with wide eyes full of questions.

He gave her his answers by capturing her lips with his own.

The kiss wasn't sweet. It was rough, passionate, and demanding. He needed her to feel what he was feeling, and he'd be damned if he'd let her leave him. Although she tried to hold her lips tightly shut, Caleb laid his hand against her face and eased her chin down with his thumb. Then he thrust his tongue into her mouth, reclaiming what he feared he'd lost.

Sara's sigh was her surrender, and he smiled against her lips, gentling the kiss and lazily stroking his tongue over hers. She slipped her arms around his waist and pressed against him. Only then, did he finally relax.

When he ended the kiss, he stared down into her eyes. "I'm sorry, Sara."

"Sorry?"

"I was an ass. I...I couldn't handle the jealousy. I was only thinking of myself, not you. Not the baby." He squeezed her hard, resting his chin on her head. "You only did what you had to. I see that now."

Her shoulders rose in an exaggerated shrug.

Caleb crooked his finger and lifted her chin. Sara was so beautiful he had to brush another kiss over her mouth. "It was all too much.

Drake came riding up, mad as a hornet, and said... He said all kinds of things."

"That's why he's here now," she said softly. "He got you all riled up and blames himself for you leaving."

"You have to understand. I was so damned happy. I had a son. Then he tells me... He says..."

"He told you the baby might be his." Sara hung her head. "We can never be sure, but—"

"Look at me."

She took her time obeying.

Holding her gaze, he said, "Don't matter to me whether that baby was born of his seed or mine. He's *my* son. He'll always be *my* son. That makes you cry?"

"Of course it makes me cry!"

"I just told you that Isaac is my son, even if Drake put him in your womb."

Her response was to cry harder.

Even if he lived to the ripe old age of sixty, Caleb would never understand women. Especially *this* woman. She'd pulled out of his arms, turning her back and crying as though she'd just buried her favorite pet.

Coming up behind her, he snaked his arms around her waist and hauled her back against him. "Why are you cryin', sweetheart?"

"I was so afraid..." A sob bubbled out.

"Afraid I wouldn't come back?"

She nodded, bumping his chin.

"But I am back, Sara. I came to my senses and I'm home."

Since she wouldn't stop crying, he figured he'd have to show her he was sincere. He ached for her, and he needed to make love to her. Now.

Without a word, Caleb swept Sara into his arms and strode to the bedroom. He kicked the door shut behind him. Then he went about the pleasurable task of removing her clothes.

She had the temerity to give him a disgruntled frown. "You can't mean to—"

"Oh, I mean to all right. I mean to hard and fast until I hear you scream my name."

Her face flushed, and her breathing sped to a faster cadence. "It's daylight."

"Yep."

"You want to...you know...in the middle of the day?"

"Yep."

Casting aside her calico dress, he flung aside his vest and jerked his own shirt over his head, not bothering to unbutton it. He knelt before her, untying the ribbons holding up her stockings, dropping them on the floor, and then slowly rolling her stockings down her sleek legs. After helping her step out of her petticoat and pantalets, he pulled her camisole off and just stared at her.

So accustomed to seeing her with Isaac in her belly, he'd forgotten how slender she was. "God, you're beautiful."

When she reached for his waistband, he smiled. She was nibbling on her bottom lip, but her nervousness didn't stop her from unbuttoning his pants and shoving them past his hips. He chuckled as he toed off his boots and then stepped out of his pants, kicking them aside.

Holding her against him, skin to skin, set his heart hammering so loudly the beat echoed in his ears. He kissed her, sliding his tongue into her mouth, caressing and showing her what he wished he could find the words to express.

But his need for her was too strong to even try to talk. Perhaps after, once he showed her what was in his heart it might be easier to tell her.

Scooping Sara into his arms, Caleb set her on the bed. He came down on top of her blanketing her body with his own, nudging her thighs apart with his knee so he could rest his cock against the curls between her thighs. "Now I'm home."

"For good?" Her gaze searched his.

He gave her a smile. "Forever."

Then he captured her mouth for a kiss, probing with his tongue until she restlessly moved against him. He trailed his kisses across her cheek, tugged on her earlobe with his teeth, and nuzzled her neck. With little bites that he soothed with gentle licks, he moved down her neck to her breast. Drawing a taut nipple between his lips, he swirled his tongue around the tight nub as she drove her fingers through his hair and tugged.

"You're making me crazy," she said, her words breathless. "I want you, Caleb."

While he wanted to tell her to be patient, he was rapidly losing his own control. So he rose over her, spreading her thighs a little farther apart before rubbing his cock against her wet, hot core.

She reached between them, wrapped her fingers around his erection, and guided him home.

The moment Caleb sank deep inside Sara, all his worries faded into nothing. Her past was gone, his stupidity forgotten. There was just his love for her and the love he knew she had for him.

He used slow thrusts to stroke her body, hoping he could hold out long enough to bring her fulfillment. It had been so long since they'd shared this intimacy. Too long.

She wouldn't let him go slow. Her hands gripped his shoulders, and she wrapped her legs around his hips. Raising her own hips each time he sank inside her, she urged him on, making him move faster. Harder. Just when he thought the battle was lost, Sara cried out, her body clenching around him. He threw his head back, shouting her name as the waves of pleasure rushed over him.

Exhausted, he collapsed against her, trying not to crush her with his weight. Sara seemed every bit as boneless, her only movement the fluttering of her fingers as she traced the length of his spine with her hand. Her legs fell to his sides, and she hummed that way she always had whenever he'd pleased her.

Now he had to find the words to tell her all that he needed her to know.

Caleb flopped to his back, still trying to catch his breath. Sara pillowed her head against his shoulder and draped her leg over his thigh.

"I'm sorry I left," he said. "I just... I needed to think things through."

"So did you think things through?" she asked. The fearful tremor in her voice reached his heart, giving him courage.

"I did. I realized one very important thing."

When he didn't say anything more, she poked his ribs. "And?"

"And I realized that no matter what happened before you knew me or how you came to me, I ain't never gonna let you go."

She propped herself on her elbow. "My past—"

"There's only now. There's only *us*," he said. "Understand?"

"Not at all."

Combing his fingers through her hair, Caleb sighed. "I ain't concerned with your past. All I care about is your future. *Our* future."

"Isaac—"

"Is my son. I'm home now, and today is a new start for us. For all three of us."

Sara rubbed her cheek against his shoulder. "I was so afraid you'd stopped loving me."

He strained his neck so he could look into her eyes. "I never stopped loving you, sweetheart. Never."

Smiling, she settled back against him.

Caleb waited for what he thought was far too long before he patted her backside. "Don't you got something to say to me now?"

"Do I?" There was a lightness to her voice that he was relieved to hear.

He growled in response.

"I love you, Caleb. With all my heart."

Chapter Twenty-Five

"In the name of the Father, the Son, and the Holy Ghost."
Reverend David punctuated each entity's invocation by pouring a small
stream of water over Isaac's forehead while Isaac accompanied each
touch of water against his skin with a shrill scream.

Caleb didn't even try to bite back his laughter, even when Sara
gave him a scolding glance. It was hard to take her scowl as a
reprimand when her own lips were twitching with a grin every time
their son wailed.

The good reverend ended the baptism by setting a white
handkerchief on Isaac's forehead. "Congratulations."

Drew, who had been standing at Caleb's side as Isaac's godfather,
cuffed Caleb on the shoulder. For once, Drew was quiet, appearing
almost choked up over the small, quiet ceremony.

Caleb inclined his head, figuring any words of thanks he gave
Drew might make the emotionally sensitive man start hugging
everyone. Again.

Cassie passed the baby back to Sara. "I'm honored to be his
godmother."

Settling Isaac in her arms, Sara smiled. "Think how much fun our
children will have as they grow up together."

Grace Morgan, her husband close on her heels, rose from her pew
and came to speak to Sara and Caleb. "I've made a cake to celebrate.
We should all head to the Four Aces to share it."

"That was mighty nice of you, Grace." He wrapped his arm around
Sara's shoulders.

"Thank you, Grace," Sara said.

When Isaac got fussy, she let Caleb take him. As usual, his son
settled down the moment Caleb laid him against his shoulder. They'd
quickly developed a father-son bond. No matter how fussy, the baby
would calm whenever he was with his father. That made Caleb happy
to the depths of his soul, and he dreamed of the things he'd teach Isaac
as the boy grew.

The most important lesson would be the importance of finding a
loving wife.

Grace gave them a smile. "It's such a special day. I wanted to help
you have a small celebration."

As Ty and Cassie joined them, Ty held his daughter, Diana, against
his shoulder the same way Caleb cradled Isaac.

Caleb kissed Isaac's temple. "You're right, Grace. Ain't every day
a man celebrates his *son's* baptism."

Ty only grinned at the teasing. "Just remember, I'll be the one holding the shotgun when your son brings his friends 'round to court my girl."

Caleb threw his head back and laughed.

***

"You truly love Caleb, don't you?" Drew asked Sara.

She just set her empty cake plate down and was preparing to start cleaning up the mess of dirty plates and forks scattered on the serving table. "'Neither rhyme nor reason can express how much.'"

He kissed her cheek and grinned. "I'm happy for you, Sara."

As fast as Caleb hurried across the room, she looked around to see if danger lurked nearby. He put himself between her and Drew and scowled. "You ain't gotta put your hands on my wife all the time." A snort slipped out. "Your lips, neither."

"Come now, Caleb," Drew said with a lopsided grin. "You're well aware that I know the depth of your feelings for our Sara." He leaned closer to Caleb. "Have you practiced the line?"

"It's s'posed to be a surprise, Drew," Caleb scolded.

"Judging from the confused look on her face, I'd say Sara is plenty surprised." Drew swept his arm toward the front of the room. "What more perfect place is there than here? What time could be more appropriate than your new son's baptism? What better audience than your family and friends?"

Caleb leaned closer to Drew and whispered, "I wanted it to be private. Not sure I can do it in front of all these folks."

Sara strained to listen in on what the men were saying. Her curiosity was on alert, and she hoped Caleb would find the courage to do whatever it was he was planning. Otherwise, she'd be hard pressed to keep from hammering him with questions on their ride home.

"Dear Caleb, 'Cowards die many times before their deaths, the valiant never taste of death but once.' Gird your loins and do this for Sara!"

Caleb thought it over a good long while. Then he shouted at his brother on the other side of the room. "Gideon! Come here!"

As Gideon strode across the room, Sara finally caught her husband's gaze. "What's going on, Caleb?"

"I–I got something I want to give you."

"But I don't need anything," she insisted.

"Didn't say you *needed* it." He passed Isaac into Gideon's arms. Then he grabbed Sara's hand and dragged her to the front of the room.

Drew clapped loudly and then waved everyone forward. "If everyone will gather 'round, Caleb has something special planned for his wife."

Her face flushed hot as the dozen or so of their family and friends came to see whatever it was Caleb had in store for her. Not used to being the center of attention, she stared at her shoes.

Cassie lightly touched her shoulder as she passed by. "Smile, Sara."

Grace and her stepdaughter, Victoria, also murmured their support as they passed her. Funny, but knowing these women were there for her meant the world to Sara, giving her courage. She straightened her spine.

No other time in her life had she felt so at home, that she belonged. To this town. To these people.

To Caleb.

With a smile, she faced him. "What exactly do you have up your sleeve, Caleb Young?"

He smiled back. "Ain't up my sleeve, sweetheart. It's in my pocket."

He fished through the breast pocket of his vest and pulled out a gold ring. Then he cleared his throat as everyone quieted down in response.

"Sara, I want to thank you for our son. I never had the chance to get you a proper wedding ring."

"I didn't ask for one," she said softly.

"That's exactly why you're so special. You ain't never asked me for nothing. You give me so much, and now I have something to offer you in return." He cleared his throat again, but then hesitated.

"Go on," Drew whispered. "You can do it."

Caleb pulled his lips into a grim line before tossing Drew a curt nod. "I got something to say to you, Sara. This is from that Shakespeare man you cotton to reading."

He was going to recite Shakespeare? Caleb hated reading. Even though he let her read to him from time to time, he said he enjoyed her voice more than the story. Yet he'd learned Shakespeare. For her.

Sara's vision blurred with tears, and she put her fingertips against her lips so she wouldn't let a sob slip out.

"This is from something called *Hamlet*. 'Doubt thou the stars are fire; doubt that the sun doth move; doubt truth to be a liar; but never doubt I love.'" He took her left hand into his and slid the ring on the third finger.

The threatening tears spilled over her lashes. "Thank you, husband."

His cheeks looked sunburned. "You're welcome, wife." Despite the accompanying catcalls and whistles, he tugged her into his arms and kissed her, long and deep. "

Then they were lost in the crowd of well-wishers.

***

"Is Isaac asleep?" Caleb asked. He'd propped the pillows against the brass headboard and kicked aside the covers.

He wasn't wearing a stitch of clothing.

"He is." She gaped at him, wondering if she'd ever grow accustomed to his handsome looks. He was a work of art, and she couldn't tear her gaze away.

One part of him began to grow, and her eyes flew wide. When she was finally to look away, she caught his smug smile.

Perhaps there was a way to wipe that smile right off his face...

Sara jerked her nightgown over her head and dropped it on the foot of the bed. She knelt on the end of the mattress before crawling toward him, kissing his feet, his strong legs, each hip. She smiled against his skin when she skipped the impudent part of him that stood ready.

He let out a frustrated groan.

The sound made her smile grow. "Since you had such a special gift for me today, I have one for you as well."

"And what would that be?"

"Something just for *you*." She wrapped her fingers around his erection and traced the length of it with her tongue.

His fingers laced through her hair, holding her someplace she loved being. His gasps and low moans urged her on, and she took him into her mouth, swirling her tongue around the cap, loving the drops of fluid coming from the slit.

Although she felt awkward, unskilled, Caleb urged her on with gasped flatteries and an appeal or two to his Maker. When he tried to drag her on top of him, she shifted out of his grasp. "Give me this, Caleb—just as you demanded of me."

He stopped fighting her and surrendered by fisting his hands in the linens. A guttural groan rumbled from his chest as he lifted his hips and came, gasping her name.

After a hasty cleanup, Sara lay in his arms. He kept humming softly, the way he often did when he was thoroughly relaxed. She ran her fingertips over his muscular stomach before tangling her fingers in the mat of dark hair on his chest. Although she knew he'd enjoyed what she'd done, she needed a few words of praise so she wouldn't feel so awkward after such an intimate encounter.

"D–did you enjoy... Oh, bother. Of course you enjoyed..." With a sigh, she laid her head on his shoulder. "Never mind."

Caleb kissed her forehead. "Sara?"

"Yes?"

"That. Was. Wonderful. Thank you."

She held her hand up. "As wonderful as my beautiful new ring?"

"Better," he murmured.

"Thank you for quoting *Hamlet*. It was quite a surprise."

He grunted and held her a little tighter.

"I have a quote for you as well," she said.

"I probably won't understand it."

"Oh, I think you will." She pushed up on her elbow so she could look into his eyes. "I remember the first time I saw you, standing there, looking so hopeful. I had one thought that day, one of the Bard's quotes that filled my head." She kissed him and then eased back. "'Who ever loved that loved not at first sight?'"

Caleb gaped at her. "Are you sayin' you loved me the first time you saw me?"

"I–I think I am. Do you know that you saved me, Caleb? If not for you—"

His fingers gently pressed against her lips. "You got it wrong. *You* saved *me*, Sara."

"I did?" she asked.

"I was nothing but a lonely man. Now I got a beautiful wife and a son. I'm happier than I ever thought I could be."

"As am I. Because for the first time in my life, I'm home."

The End

ABOUT THE AUTHOR

Author Biography:
Sandy lives in a quiet suburb of Indianapolis, where she teaches psychology. Published through Grand Central Forever Yours, Carina Press, and indie-published, she has been an Amazon #1 Bestseller multiple times and has won numerous awards including two HOLT Medallions. Please visit her website at sandyjames.com for more information or find her on Twitter and Facebook. Represented by Danielle Egan-Miller of Browne & Miller Literary.

Other Books by Sandy James:

Damaged Heroes Series
Murphy's Law (Book 1)
Free Falling (Book 2)
All the Right Reasons (Book 3)
Faith of the Heart (Book 4)
Twist of Fate (Book 5)

Safe Havens Series
Saving Grace (Book 1)
Runaway (Book 2)
Redeemed (Book 3)
Hideaway (Book 4)
False Pretenses (book 5 ~ Coming soon!)

Ladies Who Lunch Series
The Bottom Line (Book 1)
Signed, Sealed, Delivered (Book 2)
Sealing the Deal (Book 3)
Fringe Benefits (Book 4)

Alliance of the Amazons
The Reluctant Amazon (Book 1)
The Impetuous Amazon (Book 2)
The Brazen Amazon (Book 3)
The Volatile Amazon (Book 4)

Single Titles
Turning Thirty-Twelve
Rules of the Game
The Seeker

Nashville Dreams Series
Can't Walk Away (Book 1)
Can't Let Her Go (Book 2)
Can't Fight the Feeling (Book 3)

www.ingramcontent.com/pod-product-compliance
Lightning Source LLC
Chambersburg PA
CBHW060822120626
46557CB00001B/332